THE
MAD
QUEEN
OF
MORDRA

ELWY YOST

THE MAD QUEEN OF MORDRA

ELWY YOST

Cover by Laura Fernandez

Scholastic Canada Ltd.

Scholastic Canada Ltd.
123 Newkirk Road, Richmond Hill, Ontario, Canada L4C 3G5

Scholastic Inc.
730 Broadway, New York, NY 10003, USA

Ashton Scholastic Limited
Private Bag 1, Penrose, Auckland, New Zealand

Ashton Scholastic Pty Limited
PO Box 579, Gosford, NSW 2250, Australia

Scholastic Publications Ltd.
Holly Walk, Leamington Spa, Warwickshire CV32 4LS, England

Canadian Cataloguing in Publication Data

Yost, Elwy, 1925-
   The mad queen of Mordra

First ed. published under title: Billy & the
bubbleship.
ISBN 0-590-71787-1

I. Title. II. Title: Billy & the bubbleship

PS8597.O567M32 1987   jC813'.54   C87-093167-9
PZ7.Y67Ma 1987

6 5 4 3 2   Printed in Canada   1 2 3 4 5/9
                 Manufactured by Webcom Limited

With fond affection to my sons, Chris and Boz, who, when children, heard this tale of adventure told for the first time.

Contents

1
The Meteor

One crisp evening in late fall, the time when trees are bare and snow has not quite made its appearance, Billy Brown chanced upon a most astonishing discovery.

Billy lived in a great, two-storied, rambling frame house at the edge of a town called Nightcross. His room in the south wing was crammed with equipment: a junior lab, a half-built radio transmitter and his latest project, a reflector telescope which his father had helped him put together.

That night he was busy finishing up his star charts. He was, in fact, writing an entry in his notebook when it happened—a bright, blinding light flashed in his room, followed by a strange sizzling sound, like bacon frying in a pan. Billy was at his window in an instant.

There it was—a meteor, no mistaking it!—soaring over the treetops and disappearing into the woods beyond the town. And judging by the glow and the sound it was a big one!

Billy trained his telescope in the direction of the woods, but the glow had disappeared. He looked out at the homes across the back lot and listened through his partly opened window. Most of the houses were in semi-darkness. No extra lights came on, nor did he hear any unusual sounds. Clearly no one, at least not in that neighbourhood, had noticed the meteor.

He checked the digital clock beside his bed and saw that it was 10:14. It was getting late. Downstairs his mom and dad were still reading the evening paper beside an applewood fire whose warm fragrance drifted up to the landing, and in the west wing little Nancy and Steve were sound asleep. If he went down, his mom would say his imagination had been working overtime, make him some hot cocoa and send him to bed.

What to do?

Billy looked in the direction of the woods again and pondered. It was certainly late, but he didn't get the chance to pick up a meteor every day—or night. Yes, he had to investigate.

There was not a moment to lose. Quickly he threw on his jacket and scrambled out through the window onto the roof of the wide verandah. Silently he crept to the big oak at the corner of the house, grasped a limb and swung himself up into the tree. Moments later he was on the ground racing off over the back lawn and out onto Park Street.

At the first house Billy forced himself to a slower pace. He didn't want to attract attention if a neighbour happened to be looking out a window. Nothing was going to stop him from finding that meteor!

Another block and he turned right. Oak Street had a string of vacant lots and he began to sprint again. At the end was a footpath leading directly into the dark bush.

From the direction of the flash Billy was sure he knew where the meteor had landed. But now that he was in the woods, with soft moonlight filtering down through the branches casting eerie shadows all around him, he paused.

"Suppose I'm wrong," he mumbled. "Suppose it isn't a meteor. Suppose it's a ..." And while his lips didn't move, his mind formed the words *flying saucer*.

Billy froze. His eyes searched the black shapes and tangled shadows. Should he have gone downstairs and told his dad after all? What if the meteor *was* a flying saucer and he was about to meet a creature from another world? And what if that creature were hostile? His hands became fists as he thrust them deep into his pockets.

He glanced back along the path. There was still

time to go and bring his dad. Maybe they should even wait till morning when it was light and they could see what they were doing. But what if someone else had seen the meteor and got there first? No, he had to go on. There was no turning back.

As he picked his way across a gully Billy glimpsed the first traces of a glow coming through the trees. He crouched and began to feel his way through the undergrowth, moving only a few steps at a time.

The glow was blue-white and becoming brighter as he advanced. Despite the chill Billy's palms were moist, and sweat formed on his brow. He moved cautiously, letting his feet feel out every step before putting his weight down. He dared not let even the snap of a dry twig break the deadly stillness. The glow was now much stronger.

Perhaps fifty metres from the site his ears detected the frying sound he had first heard in his room. A few steps more and it was an unmistakable sizzle. And the glow appeared to be pulsating—brighter, duller, brighter, duller. It was almost as though—almost as though the meteor were mechanical!

Billy stopped ... watched ... listened.

No movement came from the clearing ahead. There was no sound of metal doors grinding open, no squeak of a hatch being raised, no shadows moving in the eerie light. Nothing but the pulsating blue-white glow coming through the trees. Quietly, nearly paralyzed with fear, Billy advanced toward the strange radiance. At last, after what seemed hours, he found himself staring into the clearing that contained the object from outer space.

What he saw immediately removed his fears about flying saucers and visitors from other worlds. It was indeed a meteor. But as Billy gazed at its pulsating glow he realized it was like no meteor he had ever heard or read about.

The object that protruded from the ground looked like an enormous chunk of ice. And like ice it was starting to melt, except that the liquid coming from it was not water. It was more like a gooey porridge, or lava, though not as thick. As Billy watched, it began to ooze its way over the grass in a narrow stream that glowed in the darkness.

For a long while he stared at this amazing sight, never so much as stirring. The meteor had almost melted to nothing when it struck Billy that he had to have proof of his discovery or no one would ever believe him. Hurriedly he began to poke around in the clearing looking for some kind of container. In a little while he found a rusty pork and bean tin, banged out the leaves and approached the edge of the meteor pit where all that was left was a pool of molten goo. Brighter, duller, brighter, duller—the strange glow continued to throb. But the precious fluid was swiftly disappearing.

Cautiously Billy kneeled on the ground, and holding the tin by its bent lid, scooped it full of the glowing substance. Then he gazed in wonder at his strange prize. The glow continued to pulse from the bean can, but he could feel no heat. The tin was as cool as the November air.

Fantastic! Billy pursed his lips and slowly shook his head. With the proof he held in his hands they would *have* to believe him. He could hardly wait to tell his father in the morning.

The pit was now almost empty and he stood and stared into it until all trace of the meteor had vanished. Soon, except for the radiance in his tin and the faint moonbeams in the trees, all was darkness in the clearing.

Billy took a last look at the dark mouth of the pit and started for home. The glow from the bean can lit his way through the bush back to Oak Street.

* * *

When Mr. and Mrs. Brown came up to bed that night they checked the children and found them, as usual, fast asleep. Billy's snores were the loudest. "My goodness that boy is sleeping soundly!" said Mr. Brown.

"It's all that fresh air he gets," whispered Billy's mother as she gently closed his bedroom door. Their footsteps disappeared down the hallway.

Quickly Billy hopped out of bed, flipped on the desk lamp and went over to the closet where he had hidden his treasure. Careful not to stumble and spill the liquid, he brought the can over to the desk and set it down beside his test tubes and chemistry set. He selected a beaker and poured some of the gooey substance into it. What a marvellous sight!

Billy turned off his lamp and stared at the miracle in his hands. In the darkened bedroom the entire beaker was alight, glowing with a cold blue radiance and pulsing regularly.

He set the beaker down, and in the eerie light began making notes. After describing the colour he timed the pulses with his watch. The regularity had been obvious to him from the start, but now, in the silence of his bedroom, he was struck by a curious coincidence: the pulse of the light in the beaker was identical to the rate of his own breathing!

It was as though the liquid light in the container were *alive!*

Billy wanted to rush out into the hall to proclaim his incredible discovery, but instead sat transfixed by the beaker, constantly checking and rechecking his observations and jotting them down in his notebook.

During the next hour he found that the more tests he did with the gooey fluid the more mysterious it became. Wearing a pair of rubber gloves, he heated some on his bunsen burner to what should have been boiling point, yet no boiling occurred. He packed a small tube of the substance in ice from the kitchen, yet found no change in the temperature. He mixed it with water, with ink, with every chemical he possessed, yet no actual mixing took place. The fluid remained exactly as it had been in the beginning. It simply sat in its container glowing and dimming, glowing and dimming, as the minutes ticked by.

On toward midnight Billy realized he had done everything except feel and taste the liquid and decided it was probably fairly safe to do so. He had earlier tested a piece of chicken meat in it and had not detected any burns or discolouring.

With extreme caution he dipped his forefinger into the fluid and to his relief experienced a pleasantly smooth sensation. When he inserted his thumb into the goo and began to rub thumb and forefinger together he experienced an even more pleasant sensation—a sort of oily softness.

Next, to get a better look at the goo while he was working it between his fingers, he got out his magnifying glass. Now he noticed that when he drew his fingers apart a thin, bluish strand stretched between them. Intrigued, he held his hand up to the light and began blowing on the almost invisible ribbon to see what would happen. The bluish thread billowed and quivered each time he blew.

Amazing!

That gave him an idea. Billy crept quietly down the hall to his brother's room. He was thankful for the dim corner light burning there because it let him find what he was looking for without too much noise. In a few moments he was back in his own room seated before the glowing beaker.

What he had brought with him from his brother's play table was a plastic loop used for blowing soap bubbles. "Well, here goes," he whispered as he dipped it into the beaker, withdrew it and then blew.

A shimmering bubble about the size of a grapefruit suddenly was there in front of him, floating in mid-air above the surface of the desk. Billy was delighted. He prodded it with his finger, but it didn't pop the way soap bubbles do. He puffed at it, but it didn't float away. It just hovered there, motionless.

He poked the bubble harder and marvelled that his finger could enter without bursting it. Even when he wiggled his finger the bubble still didn't break.

This gave Billy another idea. He reached over, picked up a marble knight from the chess board beside his bed and eased it inside. He was amazed to find that it felt almost weightless. Scarcely daring to breathe, and risking a loud clatter if it fell to the desk top, he let go.

It didn't fall! The knight stayed there, supported by the inner surface of the sphere, floating mysteriously in the bluish light.

Billy took out the chess piece and put it back on the board. He dipped his finger in the beaker once again, then touched the bubble. In a flash it shrank to a tiny bead of fluid shimmering on his fingertip.

He leaned back in his chair and rubbed his fingers together. What kind of bubble would he get if he blew a little harder? He dipped the loop into the glowing beaker, held it close to his lips, took a deep breath and . . .

He couldn't believe his eyes! But it was true. Hovering gently before him was an enormous bubble, taller even than he was, and faintly shimmering with an unearthly light.

2

The Bubble

Cautiously Billy reached out to touch the surface of the bubble. As before, there was only a slight resistance and then his hand passed right through. When he withdrew it he noticed that none of the goo had stuck to his skin. Interesting! Finally he poked his head in. Again he experienced almost no sensation and again it didn't burst.

There was only one thing left: Billy stepped boldly inside the bubble. To his amazement he found himself floating a few centimetres above the floor!

His first reaction was to put one foot forward in a bracing action to prevent himself from falling, but he needn't have bothered. He was quite upright and secure, even though the feeling under his feet was most peculiar. It was as though he were standing on a thick, spongy carpet of air. A trampoline was the nearest comparison he could think of. When he reached out to touch the walls of the bubble, he felt the same spongy resistance.

A momentary panic struck him as it occurred to him that he might be trapped inside the bubble. He pressed outward with his arms, even using his shoulders and legs, but the filmy material was tough and strong. It stretched the way an elastic would, but did not split or pop. In desperation he made a sharp, sideways movement with his body and suddenly found himself standing once more on the floor of his room.

Billy gave a sigh of relief. The bubble was unchanged, a shimmering globe of blue light still hovering in the same spot.

What else would it do? he wondered. So far it hadn't moved. What would it be like to stand inside and float across the floor to his bed? No harm in trying. Besides, he was too caught up in his experiments to stop. He stepped back into the bubble and a moment later discovered it possessed another amazing property. By simply *wanting* to float across the floor Billy found that the bubble moved in an effortless, graceful glide entirely as he wished.

Fantastic! It was like having his own airplane right in his room!

A little later Billy opened his bedroom door and began floating along the corridor past where his mom and dad were sleeping and past Steve's and

Nancy's rooms. If they could only see me now, he thought, how amazed they would be!

His next move was to float down the staircase into the lower part of the house where he sailed into the kitchen, through the dining room and on into the living room. He hovered in front of the aquarium where the goldfish stared at him with unblinking eyes . . . he floated up to the ceiling . . . he sailed over the sofa and chairs.

He was having such fun that he scarcely noticed how swiftly time was slipping by, but when the cuckoo clock in the family room chirped one, he knew he simply had to get to bed. He soared back upstairs to his bedroom and stepped out of the bubble. In the soft light of the desk lamp it looked so beautiful and fragile that Billy could not bring himself to dissolve it.

I should leave it the way it is anyway, he thought, just to see how long it will last. He pushed it gently into the corner, hoping it would still be there in the morning. Then he opened his window a little, because he preferred to sleep under sub-arctic conditions, turned off the lamp and jumped into bed.

But sleep wouldn't come. Billy was too excited. Lying on his side, eyes wide open, he stared at the moonlight streaming through the window.

After a while he became aware of something very

odd. The moonlight seemed to be blue!

Feeling a little uneasy he slipped out of bed and walked over to the gently stirring curtains. But at the window he discovered there was a very practical explanation for the blue colour. His bubble had covered most of the glass and seemed to be hugging the narrow opening. Billy closed the window and steered it over to the far corner again. Imagine that! he thought. His bubble was actually trying to get out!

Instead of returning to bed he went back to the window and gazed out over the sloping verandah roof. What a beautiful night! And how lovely the bubble had looked, bathed in the moonbeams coming into the room. He stood there for a long time musing, reliving the events of the evening and wondering where the bubble might be trying to escape to.

"One thing for sure," he murmured, "I'll never need to shinny up or down that oak tree anymore. From now on I'll fly." He imagined himself out on the roof taking off in the bubble and floating down through the trees for a perfect landing on the grass below. He saw himself zooming up over the housetops, maybe out to Park Street or Oak Street, even over Alan and Jerry's house. He chuckled as his mind's eye caught the startled expressions on his friends' faces as they looked out of their window and saw Billy Brown in a bubble sailing past the moon.

Gosh, he thought, I'll try it! Tomorrow night after everyone's gone to sleep I'll open the window wide and fly out. I'll soar over the trees and rooftops! I can always tell Mom and Dad the next day. I'll keep the bubble a secret for just one more night.

Smiling to himself, he crawled into bed and fell fast asleep.

*   *   *

All Saturday Billy could hardly wait for evening to come. During the morning, each time he went to his bedroom he cast an anxious eye into the dark closet where he had hidden the bubble and the beaker of goo. The afternoon was even more frustrating because Mom and Dad insisted on taking the entire family over to Grandma Brown's for dinner. But at last night fell and the family returned home.

Billy had his bath and snuggled under the covers. His room was dark save for the moonlight from the window and the numbers on his digital clock, which glowed in the inky gloom. 9:15. Billy chuckled. Not yet time. But soon, very soon, it would be.

Presently Mom came in all dressed up, gave his blankets a final tuck around his neck and kissed his cheek. She and Dad were off to a meeting of the Cross Country Skiing Association at the high school and Dad was already outside getting the car started. With a "Sweet dreams" she closed the door softly behind her.

Marianne, the family babysitter, wouldn't be checking on Billy till after ten, so he had most of an hour. He got out of bed and slipped on his denims, sneakers, T-shirt and suede jacket. Then he opened the closet, let his blue bubble float into the room and took down the precious beaker. He poured some goo into his empty water canteen and attached it to his belt. He wanted to be sure he had a good supply on hand in case the bubble broke. Then he put the beaker back up on his closet shelf, making sure it was well hidden, and shoved the plastic loop into his pocket. The clock read 9:25.

Time to go!

Billy threw open his window and stepped into the bubble, biting his lip in anticipation of the sheer drop down the side of the verandah. To his relief the bubble simply glided out through the window and over the patches of moonlight under the limbs of the giant oak tree.

What a marvellous sensation! Skiing couldn't come near it. He zoomed down toward the grass, levelled off and was just beginning mentally to guide his craft toward Alan and Jerry's place when a remarkable thing happened. Free of the shadows of the oak tree, the bubble seemed suddenly to be possessed of a mind of its own!

Billy was almost shaken off his feet as it shot straight up into the open path of moonlight. The Brown house and the old oak tree dropped away as the bubble soared into the sky. Then, as though it were taking its second wind, it swooped down in a long glide, coming within a treetop's distance of Park Street before rising again.

Billy glanced toward the pavement and spied the family car speeding on its way to the high school. In the glow of the dashboard he could just barely make out the faces of his mom and dad as his sphere sped past and began to climb. What would they see, what would they think if they just happened to glance up into the sky? But they were too busy chatting—and so missed the view of a lifetime.

Now Billy was moving at a truly alarming rate. He closed his eyes and concentrated with all his might, but it had no effect whatever on the blue bubble. Faster and faster it rose into the night sky. Soon all the lights in Nightcross, the house lights, the street lamps, the traffic lights, lay like a cluster of stars in the dark countryside tumbling away below him.

The moonlight grew brighter and more dazzling and the bubble, throbbing as never before, became a pure radiant blue.

Billy's heart was in his mouth. Why had he attempted this mad experiment all by himself? Why hadn't he done as he had originally planned and shared the whole strange discovery with his dad? Why hadn't he taken Alan and Jerry into his confidence so they, at least, would know what had happened to him? Now no one knew! He was vanishing clear off the face of the Earth and nobody knew where he was going or what would become of him!

The bright disc of the moon grew larger and larger every second. The speed at which he was travelling was terrifying. There was now no trace of Nightcross or even of the Earth below him. All he was conscious of was the moon's rapidly expanding face and the light flooding his eyes.

Then, abruptly, the moon fell away and Billy Brown saw the vast floor of the universe spread out before him. Except for the stars, which were like grains of scattered salt, all was darkness. Out of nowhere, an area blacker than pitch suddenly loomed ahead.

As the bubble approached this inky pit it went into orbit around it, forming great circles that became smaller and smaller as the sphere went faster and faster. As it was drawn closer toward the centre Billy remembered something from his star books and his mind filled with horror!

Directly below him, and only moments away, was a *black hole*—and he was heading right into it!

3
The Golden Glove

When Billy regained consciousness he found he was still inside the bubble. But he was now racing through misty banks of cloud and there was no sign of the black hole. Had he actually gone through it?

He felt he had been away from home for hours and glanced at his watch. It registered 9:35. That was odd. He had left home at 9:25. Surely he had been gone a lot longer than ten minutes. Or was it already the next morning? Billy was certain he had not been gone as long as twelve hours.

Where had the black hole carried him? It was unlike any black hole he had ever read about. If it had been, he would have been squashed to the size of an atom.

The bubble continued to make its way through the thick mists whirling around it, and a little while later Billy checked his watch again. It still read 9:35. He whacked it a couple of times in the palm of his hand. No luck. As he might have suspected, it had gone on the blink. He had no way of knowing how long he had been away from home. Why, oh why, did it have to conk out at a time like this?

At that moment there was a shimmering of light ahead, and before Billy knew it he was out of the cloud bank and soaring through an incredibly blue sky. He couldn't tell what was directly below him—perhaps it was an ocean—but there was no mistaking what was in front of him.

On either side, as far as he could see, rose a wall of mountains. He had never, even on his trips to British Columbia, seen mountains like these—so huge, with such tall, spindly tops, and yet so smooth and rounded, with no sharp peaks or crags. And the broad slopes and valleys were covered in snow—a pale blue snow, not at all like the snow back home in Nightcross.

Where was he?

A coastline slid into view and at that point, as though by signal, the bubble started to slow down. From the time Billy had left Nightcross he had been flying in a sphere that was definitely not under his control, but now all of a sudden he had only to will the bubble to do as he wished and it obeyed. He was in charge again, and he liked that very much.

The first thing he did was direct it down toward the coast. He knew mountains could be terrible places to get lost in, but a seashore might have ports and ports would mean people. As his bubble descended Billy cast his eyes up and down the coastline, but there was no sign whatever that human beings lived in this strange-looking world.

All at once his attention was caught by what seemed to be a long black thread twisting down a mountain slope all the way to the sea. At first he thought it might be a dry river bed, but then it occurred to him that a river running down a mountain wouldn't have quite so many curves. In a flash he realized what it must be.

A road! It could only be a road!

Billy dropped to a lower altitude so he could get a better look at his marvellous discovery. A road had to connect with people. All he had to do was follow it. He clapped his hands together as he continued his descent.

But at the coast the road ended in a most peculiar way. It ran right into the sea! Billy was dumbfounded.

He landed the bubble near the water's edge and stepped out onto the smooth, hard surface of the road. He waded out a short distance ... and then it struck him. Here he was, walking in an ocean in wintertime, and it wasn't even cold! In fact it was pleasantly warm. Not only that, but he was standing on a road that was running along the bottom of a sea!

Billy crouched down and ducked his head under

the surface, but he couldn't see very well. He was about to duck under a second time when something caught his eye. In the near distance a black object was moving across the snow. As Billy stared, it disappeared. No! There it was again! It reappeared briefly, rounding a curve, only to disappear once more behind one of the endless mountain contours. It seemed to be a machine of some kind and it was approaching rapidly.

Quickly Billy waded ashore and hid with his bubble behind some large boulders. Here he would not be seen but he could get a good look at the strange machine heading in his direction. Soundlessly it glided down the last long grade of the road and came to a halt directly at the water's edge. Billy kept his head well down, peering cautiously at the huge vehicle through a small gap between two boulders. He gasped.

The sleek, low-slung body was supported by skis that did not come into contact with the road. Like a hovercraft it seemed to be floating on a narrow cushion of air, but there was no sound of motors, no whirling dust or spray.

All at once a side panel slid open and a tall man wearing high boots and dressed from head to toe in black stepped out. He had a long, narrow face, a narrow nose, narrow eyes and a thin black moustache. A loose, flowing cape hung from his shoulders and in one gloved hand he carried a riding crop, which he continually whacked into the open palm of the other. He seemed very impatient.

A second person joined him from the interior of the car. It was a boy who looked slightly younger than Billy, with the reddest hair Billy had ever seen. He was dressed in a white blouse, green breeches and dark brown boots. And he wore a pair of exquisitely beautiful golden-coloured gloves.

The man seemed to take exception to the presence of the boy outside the cab, for he spoke curtly to him in a language Billy didn't understand and motioned him to get back into the vehicle. The boy ignored the command and took a pace or two into the water, staring solemnly out to sea.

But the dark man was not to be disobeyed. He gave his open gloved hand a terrific whack and called sharply. He was striding toward the boy when a sudden loud whooshing of water stopped him. A second machine surfaced from the sunken road in front of them.

Billy stared in wonder as two men in broad black hats and large capes waded ashore. The tall man gave them a slight nod. Then he placed his gloved hands on the boy's shoulders and began to guide him through the water toward the two newcomers.

But the red-haired boy would have none of it. He yelled something and squirmed loose. Horrified,

Billy saw that he was running straight to his own hiding place!

Just as the boy reached the tumble of boulders and began scrambling over them, the man was upon him, trying to pull him back. The boy was strong and put up a terrific fight. Kicking furiously, he clung to a corner of rock directly above Billy's head. In the scuffle he pulled himself up over the edge of the boulder, and for one brief moment the eyes of the two boys met. Then the tall man pulled him loose with such force that his hand came flying out of his glove.

There were more yells and the clatter of hard boots on stone, followed by a dull thud. Then dead silence.

When Billy worked up enough courage to peer through the rocks again he saw the two men in capes carrying the boy toward the machine that lay half submerged in the water. The tall man remained on the shore watching until the second machine had turned around and disappeared below the surface. Then he returned to his ski-car, stepped inside and uttered a command to an unseen driver. Seconds later the long black vehicle was gliding back up the mountain road.

For many long moments afterward Billy just sat behind the boulders, puzzled and shaken by the strange and violent events that had taken place. It was only when he climbed to his feet and started to get into his bubble that he noticed the golden glove still clinging to the rock.

*   *   *

High above the mountain valley, keeping his bubble well behind the ski-car, Billy followed the progress of the tall man. He was the very last person Billy wanted to meet face to face, but he had to make contact with *someone* and following him seemed the only way. Billy looked at the beautiful golden glove which he clutched in his right hand. If he could just find someone who knew the boy, or at least knew of him, he might be able to find his parents . . .

But wait a minute! What was happening down below?

Billy snapped back from his pondering and stared at the mountain road twisting far beneath his bubble. Something akin to panic seized him.

Where was the ski-car? It had completely disappeared from sight!

In a burst of speed he guided the bubble down to road level and began to race in the direction the black vehicle had been heading. As each bend unfolded before him there was nothing ahead except another bend. There must have been a fork in the highway, he decided, wondering how he could possibly have missed it.

Billy was about to retrace his route when, glancing up, he discovered he was hovering at the base of a most amazing range of mountains—quite the largest and highest he had yet encountered. He zoomed upwards in order to get a better view. Incredible! The summits must have been at least five times as high as Mount Everest, they were so dimly visible. He thought it odd he hadn't noticed their approach. He must have been too buried in his own thoughts.

Billy studied the high slopes, but could detect no movement nor any sign of the roadway. As his eyes scanned the blue-white snow and rocky outcroppings, it suddenly dawned on him that the situation here was probably much the same as in Canada. If a road didn't go over a mountain, it went through it. Of course, that was the answer!

He dropped back down to the road and continued in the direction he had been following. It was not long before he found where the vehicle had vanished. Around a final bend yawned the black mouth of a tunnel.

Billy floated up to the entrance with extreme caution. There was always the possibility that his pursuit of the ski-car had already been detected by its two occupants. But all looked clear. Far ahead and swiftly receding down the tunnel, whose walls were faintly luminous, was a barely visible dot which must be the ski-car. Thank goodness he hadn't lost it!

4

The Ice-Gun

The mountain range must have been of an immense girth because the tunnel didn't seem to have an end. It descended so steeply that Billy figured he must be passing well below sea level. He checked his watch, but he might have known it was useless. It still registered 9:35. There was no way of telling how long he had been travelling down the tunnel. It seemed like an hour, yet it could have been two.

What greeted him when he emerged into the daylight could not have been more surprising. All around him, rising layer upon layer to incredible heights, was a dense and monstrous jungle. Trees with trunks the thickness of houses rose high into the air, their limbs bearded with vines and moss and broad enough for an army to march along. Profusions of brightly coloured flowers dotted the wall of green forest and extended even to the uppermost reaches, where a canopy of lush vegetation spread in waves into the distance. At ground level grew long, deep grass and canes, and between the tree trunks at the edge of the forest no light penetrated the dark green depths.

It was a spectacular and beautiful sight, but at the same time strange, unreal and very eerie.

Perhaps eeriest of all was the way the mountain road behaved. As though taking its cue from the tall vegetation, the highway climbed steeply and curved off through the tree boughs which supported it. Billy imagined that a ride along that thoroughfare would be like a ride on a roller coaster.

But the ski-car—where was it?

Quickly Billy guided his bubble up along the skyroad and entered the gloom of the great jungle. There was no sign of the black vehicle anywhere, only the empty road undulating off into the dank background, swooping up over giant limbs and curving sharply around solitary tree trunks. He knew it *had* to be somewhere up ahead. His pace was swift and steady, and the great dips and sweeps almost took his breath away.

He had not travelled far when he spied the ominous ski-car at the base of a broad dip in the skyway. It was parked and its panel door was wide open. Puzzled, Billy guided his bubble behind a great moss-coated limb to one side of the road and surveyed the machine carefully. Why would it be parked where it was, and where were the tall man and his driver?

A quick scan below the road gave Billy his answer. From the side of the skyway a ladder dropped down to the jungle floor beneath. There, in a shaft of light that streaked through an opening in the trees, two dark figures knelt together by a stream, drinking water from cups and chatting. Billy was too far away to see clearly, but he knew it had to be the tall man and his driver.

This was his chance! Before they climbed back up the ladder he could take a quick look inside the ski-car. There might be something stowed away in a glove compartment—maybe even a map of some kind. Anything he could lay his hands on would be useful.

Billy knew he wouldn't have much time and would have to keep a very careful check on the two by the stream. Gently, keeping the skyroad between himself and the pair below, he moved his bubble behind a cluster of branches near the ski-car. Then he jumped out and peered over the edge of the road. Through a blur of leaves he could still see the two men huddled in conversation. But he would have to move quickly.

He ran his fingers along the black metallic surface of the car. It was uncannily smooth. Grasping the handles on either side of the opening, he pulled himself up and stepped gingerly inside.

In an instant the door slammed shut!

Billy spun around and came face to face with someone emerging from the shadows in the far interior of the car. It was the tall, dark man with the narrow face!

Billy froze, transfixed by the man's green eyes. When those eyes came closer and peered with intense suspicion into his own, Billy knew he was staring at the most terribly evil face he had ever seen.

The tall man reached out and gripped Billy's shoulders like a steel clamp.

"Tel anna?" he barked in a dry, hard voice. His tone made the meaning clear. He was asking Billy who he was.

In a torrent of words that jumbled one on top of the other like spilled marbles, he explained that his name was Billy Brown and that he was from a town called Nightcross in a province called Ontario in a country called Canada on a planet called Earth and that Earth was in the Solar System and that the Solar System was in the Milky Way.

The man shook his head in amazement. Obviously he couldn't understand a word, but he did seem to sense that Billy was a stranger from another world.

A smile crept across his narrow face and his green

eyes glinted in wonder. He relaxed his grip on the boy's shoulders, stepped back a pace and examined Billy's clothing from head to toe, occasionally touching the fabric of his T-shirt, suede jacket and blue denims. Even the boy's white sneakers absorbed his interest. But his face darkened suddenly when he noticed the golden glove clutched tightly in Billy's hand.

He uttered something that sounded like "*Sen dava!*"—it must have been an oath—snatched the glove and flung it onto a rear seat. Then he slid back the panel door and pushed Billy brusquely outside.

The tall man's two companions were not long in climbing up the ladder from the jungle floor. When they caught sight of Billy they whispered "Oooh" and "Ahhh" and began circling him, touching various parts of his clothing the way their leader had done.

Billy's greatest fear was that his canteen containing the precious fluid would be discovered, and when one of the men demanded that he unbuckle it from his belt and hand it over, his heart sank. He couldn't have been more surprised when, after pouring a few drops on his fingers and sniffing the substance, the man handed the canteen back, nodding and commenting casually in a tone that suggested the fluid was of no importance.

The miraculous goo seemed to be familiar to the three men and considered quite ordinary. Bewildering though this was, Billy was convinced they would not have acted so casually had they known about the bubbles the gooey liquid could produce. He took a sidelong glance and noted the faint blue sheen of his bubble still hovering where he had left it deep in the shadows.

The tall man went back inside the car and reappeared with the golden glove clasped in his hand. The other two joined him, speaking in low voices and occasionally glancing from the glove to the boy. They were obviously puzzled about how Billy had followed them, but the question that seemed uppermost in their minds was what to do with the young, blond-haired stranger. *Something* had to be done with him—he knew too much. But *what?*

While the three discussed Billy's fate, he looked sideways toward the bubble and mentally commanded it to ease itself forward. It had always obeyed him when he was inside it. Now he prayed he could control it from the outside.

The bubble shimmered in the darkness of the branches and slipped forward, keeping to one side of the roadway as though it were as cautious and nervous of being detected as Billy was. The magic of the bubble never ceased to amaze him. All he had to do was *want* it to do something and it did it. It was as though the bubble were somehow part of him.

Billy commanded it to dip down beneath the edge of the skyway and glide to a position just below him. This it did, and within moments it was hanging in shimmering iridescence just out of sight of the three men by the ski-car.

Billy waited for the right moment, praying that the bubble was strong enough to take the weight of his body as he plunged. If it didn't he would never get a second chance.

Any second now, he thought as he edged his way closer, idly toying with some leaves and gazing casually at the giant tree limbs above.

Now! Ready . . . set . . . jump!

But before he could move, a hand clasped the back of his neck and a voice barked, *"Pren gallor fancee!"*

Billy shuddered and turned to look up at the tall man, who was pointing at his canteen and making an impatient gesture with the golden glove.

Once more he unbuckled his container and handed it over. Again he was careful not to look concerned, but in his heart was a sickening feeling at having to part, even temporarily, with his meteor liquid. To be without it would mean that if anything happened to the bubble there would be no way of getting back home, let alone escaping.

The tall man went to the ski-car and tossed the

container inside. Was he still puzzled about how Billy had managed to follow them, and had he decided to re-examine the precious goo? There was no way of telling.

Below, the blue bubble appeared to shimmer impatiently, almost as though it were waiting for Billy to make his move.

What was he to do now?

One of the men reached into the vehicle and withdrew what appeared to be a flashlight. It was long and black, with a glassy end and a row of red and white buttons along the top. The leader and the other man watched with amusement while their companion directed the instrument toward a bird sitting on a branch above them grooming its feathers. Suddenly a beam of white light shot from the flashlight. The bird seemed to glow for a moment, then stopped grooming. In fact, it stopped moving altogether and just sat on the limb as if stunned—or frozen!

The tall man reached up and shook the end of the branch. The bird tumbled off its perch and fell to the roadway where it broke into a hundred pieces, as though it were made of glass. Billy winced and swallowed hard, his breath coming in nervous pants. These reactions did not go unnoticed, for the three men looked at him and began to laugh.

Then the leader grew stern, took the ice-gun from

the other man and approached Billy.

The rest was a nightmare!

Billy's body unwound like a watch spring. He snatched the golden glove from the tall man's hand —momentarily surprising his captor—and shot off the edge of the skyway. Overhead, a white ray flashed, turning a cluster of leaves into a tinkling chandelier.

The bubble was waiting and caught the boy gently as he fell. He bounced, somersaulted and quickly pulled himself into a crouching position. A second later he was racing off between the curved boughs of the trees.

Above and behind him the tall man and his two companions were dashing around in a frenzy, rushing to the brink of the skyway and yelling at the top of their lungs.

Billy glanced back through the maze of limbs and vines and caught a jerky image of the tall man kneeling in order to get a better aim with his ice-gun.

One ... two ... three ... four ... five bursts of white light flashed past Billy, narrowly missing him. To come so close to his target amid such a profusion of soaring tree limbs, the man must have been an amazing marksman.

Billy knew he was almost out of sight because he could now only barely make out the three men through the trees.

Then came a sixth blast of light! To Billy's horror the entire bubble lit up like a gigantic neon sign. The tips of his fingers, pressing against the inside surface, suddenly became dead cold, as though frost-bitten, and he moaned in pain. But what was worse was the realization that the bubble had lost its spongy, rubbery texture and had been transformed into a hollow ball of glass!

Or *ice!*

The marksman had made a direct hit!

The magic went out of the blue bubble. Like a light bulb flung from a cliff it spun over and over, carrying Billy with it.

5
The Jungle

A dull, hollow *boom* was followed by a shower of splintered ice as the bubble collided with a tree bough and catapulted Billy head over heels into a nest of vines and leaves.

He was back on his feet in seconds. Looking out from his perch he saw the three men running along a massive limb in his direction, the tall one in the lead shouting, "*Kon odor ... kon odor!*" Plainly the words meant, "I hit him ... I hit him!"

Billy had to move swiftly. He had no desire to become a human popsicle.

Stuffing the golden glove inside his belt, he started running along the limb he had fallen on. The boughs swooped and dipped in steep curves far above the ground. A bad stumble would mean disaster. The leaps from one bough to the next were tricky—a jump too far or too short and all would be over for Billy Brown. Once during the early stages of his flight he found himself at a dead end and might have been trapped if it hadn't been for a convenient vine that allowed him to shinny down to the limb below.

He was running like a circus acrobat on a high wire. The three pursuers were in excellent physical condition and they were in territory that was familiar to them, but minute by minute Billy was gaining ground—and time. Finally the tall man was forced to return to his ski-car and make other plans for the boy's capture. He was not going to catch up to him on foot in this wilderness.

For the first half hour of flight Billy's route had been determined as much by luck as by quick thinking. Gradually, however, he became aware, from the way the moss was worn away and the tree bark smoothed and flattened, that he was following a kind of path through the tree boughs that animals— or people?—had been taking for a long time.

At length he arrived on a limb high above a river with no way he could immediately see of getting to the other side. What strange creatures might be lying in wait beneath the surface of the water should he try to swim across? Then Billy caught sight of several long, slender vines resembling well-used ropes, moored to an enormous tree by grass cords. Above, the vines stretched a hundred metres to the tip of a great branch extending out to mid-river.

Billy looked around. He was standing on what

appeared to be a launching ramp, but the prospect of the gigantic swing he would have to make to cross the river was dizzying. From his present height above the water, the position of the high limb over the river and the incredible length of the vines, he was certain that his body would be travelling at an appalling speed.

But the idea of the drop was even more terrifying. Reluctantly he decided to follow the river downstream. Then the obvious struck him. He would *have* to make the crossing. There was really no other choice. Only by following the trail did he stand a chance of making contact with other human beings.

Without looking down, without daring to think of the violent speed of descent, Billy resolutely seized one of the vines and withdrew it from its moorings. Gripping it firmly with both hands and taking a deep breath, he closed his eyes and jumped.

The plunge made him feel that his stomach was left behind on the platform. If he had had any real notion of what it would be like he would have followed his earlier instinct and gone downriver. Only the vine and its tugging reminder that it was working against gravity saved him from absolute panic. His senses told him he was rushing headlong into the river at a speed and angle that would flatten him like a pancake once he hit its brown surface.

Death seemed imminent.

For a split second Billy opened his eyes. He couldn't help it. His body was roaring downward between branches and leaves and the river was leaping up to meet him. He had thought that skiing on the big slopes behind Nightcross was the fastest his body could ever go, but he was wrong. This was infinitely worse.

As he rushed toward the water Billy clamped his eyes shut again. But when, a fraction of a second later, he found that no impact had taken place, he opened them to discover that he was skimming just above the surface like an airplane about to land. No —it was like an airplane about to take off! In another second he was soaring upward toward a black wall of jungle towering high overhead. The climb steepened sharply and swiftly until Billy realized he was flying almost straight up!

How could he possibly make a landing like this?

Whooshhh! The terror that had gripped him suddenly subsided as he shot into a narrow gap and began to slow down. A moment later Billy let go of the vine and tumbled onto the safety of a giant bough.

"Zoweee!" he shouted as he got to his feet and looked back at the way he had come. What a crossing! He took a deep breath and sighed with relief.

But there was no time to waste. He set off at a

swift pace along his new tree-top highway, noting that it was even more worn here than on the other side of the river. He knew he must be getting close to some kind of civilization and wondered if the people living there would be anything like the tall man in black.

Rays of light shafted downward in a kind of smoky haze, brightening Billy's journey through the dark shadows of the trees. Here and there, where there was more light than in other places, the vegetation was lush, but nowhere was there any sign of snakes or other wild creatures—except for flocks of brightly coloured birds.

Presently the trees began to thin out and Billy discovered he had arrived at another dead end. He found himself at the very edge of the jungle, standing on a large platform made of logs lashed together by grass rope. Above and beyond, the sky was a brilliant blue, with no clouds anywhere in sight. Below and beyond, as far as the eye could see, stretched a vast and dismal swampland. It seemed like the end of the world! Billy's heart sank with the awful realization that there was nowhere to go but back.

The discovery of a trough of food extending along one side of the platform did not do much to cheer his spirits. He sat down cross-legged and nibbled at the chunks of bread, fruit and nuts, taking an occasional sip of the water that was also provided.

As Billy poked at his meal it occurred to him that he had been through a great deal that day and that he should have been a lot hungrier than he actually was. Come to think of it, if the day had been so long, why wasn't it getting dark? The bright blue sky hadn't changed in the slightest since he had first broken through the misty bank of clouds.

There had to be answers to these questions. There seemed to be a fresh mystery every time he turned around—like the very next moment when he decided to lie back on the platform and have a nap. He had no sooner got into position, rolling up his suede jacket for a pillow, when it struck him that he really wasn't very tired.

And yet he should have been exhausted. He had travelled such a long, long way. Back home in Nightcross he would have been on the sofa by now, in front of the TV, having a little snooze. He *had* to be tired—so much had happened. But he wasn't. Even when he rolled over on his side and closed his eyes he didn't feel the slightest bit drowsy.

Something was wrong! Billy pinched himself to make sure he wasn't dreaming and began shaking his head. Everything seemed so real and yet . . .

Take this log platform, for instance. It seemed to

be a very solid, very practical structure. What was it doing way out here in the middle of nowhere? It would have made a good landing site for helicopters, but what were the fruit, bread and nuts for?

Billy was inspecting a section of the grass rope that bound the logs together, noting how intricately it had been woven, when something curious began to happen. His shadow had started to grow! Little by little it was expanding all around him!

He quickly clasped his hands together, touched his face and chest, and slowly got to his knees. He was all right. Nothing had changed.

But his shadow had! It was quite large and becoming larger and more ominous by the second!

Billy looked up in alarm and shuddered! Hovering soundlessly above him was a gigantic bird with the eyes and beak of a hawk. It was darting wicked glances at him as its huge claws reached down.

Billy was paralyzed. Even if there had been any place to hide, he couldn't have moved his legs. He had never seen anything quite so horrifying in all his life. He sank to the floor of the platform, frozen in terror, and waited for the enormous creature to sink its claws into his trembling flesh. He didn't even have the strength to yell.

Soundlessly, with the barest movement of its vast wings, the bird slipped downward and alighted on the platform. Ignoring Billy, it hopped over to the trough and began to peck at the nuts and fruit. Occasionally its feathers would brush against him, but the brush was gentle.

Since the bird continued to eat, paying not the slightest attention to him, Billy's confidence gradually returned and he rose to his feet. It was then that he spied something on the bird's feathery back, just behind the neck. It was oddly shaped and strangely coloured, but unmistakable. A *saddle!* A saddle with *stirrups!*

In whatever weird world Billy had landed—and it was getting weirder by the moment—this giant bird was a domestic creature. All fear vanished and he managed a faint smile. Standing before him was a gentle beast of burden, not quite as handsome as his horse Maud up on his grandfather's farm, but possibly just as obliging.

It had *come* from some place and it was *heading* someplace and Billy was going to find out where. It would be a flight of mystery, but then hardly more mysterious than the whole trip had been so far. And perhaps, just perhaps, at the end of it would be a corral like the one Maud was used to, and maybe someone who could help him.

When the giant hawk had finished its meal it turned and hopped toward Billy, tucking in its wings and bowing its head. Mounting the great creature suddenly seemed the most natural thing in the world.

A moment later, with a marvellous undulation of wings, the bird—and Billy—were airborne.

6
The Tree People

Fortunately for Billy the flight from Nightcross had accustomed him to dizzying heights. Otherwise the journey on the back of the hawk would have turned his stomach.

The great bird swooped and soared in breathtaking curves over the swampland, but for Billy it was the ride of his life. There were no reins to hold onto, so he simply gripped the saddle bow and crouched close to the hawk's back. After the first glide, which was long and swift, came the heavy flap of wings and the slow climb to a lofty height from where he could see the river he had crossed and beyond that, over the tall jungle, the mountain barrier he had passed through.

Indeed, as Billy scanned the horizon he could see mountains in all directions. At one point he caught a glimpse of rolling sand dunes and a lake, but the bird wasn't heading in that direction. Their destination was an island of trees that stood far out on the marsh.

Soon the bird was gliding toward a landing platform. It swooped almost to a complete standstill, then hovered lightly for a moment before settling. When Billy dismounted he patted its feathery back, walked around to the head that earlier had been so ugly and frightening and gently stroked its neck. A hooded green eye blinked at the boy and a soft *coo* came from the curved beak. Well, thought Billy, at least I have *one* friend.

Once again he was off along a tree bough, wondering where it was going to lead him. This time he did not have far to go.

Up on his right, poised at the top of a steep limb in which steps had been carved, was an oddly shaped house with a verandah running all the way around it. It had no chimney, but it did have open windows and a round, open doorway. A shaft of hazy light fell across its thatched roof and made it seem warm and cheery.

As Billy peered into the jungle around him other houses, some much higher and some far lower, popped into view. He suddenly realized he was standing in the middle of a village of tree dwellings perched high above the jungle floor. They all looked cozy and inviting, although there was not a single person in sight. Just the same, thought Billy, human beings could not be very far away.

A gentle tinkling of bells began to sound. It came from everywhere at once and lasted for about a minute before it faded away. Immediately he was aware of movement here and there among the boughs and soon figures emerged into view—mostly men, a few women and some children, all dressed in varying shades of green. As they gathered around him everyone stared at Billy with an expression of curiosity and amazement, but there was a gentleness and ease in the way they looked that put his mind immediately at rest.

"*Tel anna?*" one of them said, stepping forward, and Billy knew he was being asked who he was. The man was quite handsome: tall, with light brown skin and dark brown curly hair. He placed his right hand on Billy's left shoulder, and Billy thought he had better do the same. A murmur of approval ran through the crowd.

"*Tel anna?*" Billy repeated, looking up into the brown man's face and mustering a faint grin. The man nodded agreeably and replied something that sounded like *Yan*. Then Billy pronounced his own name and stated where he had come from, but before he had got very far a roar of laughter broke out. Billy had never thought his voice sounded funny, but apparently everyone here did. Realizing they couldn't understand a word he said, he finished by making long gestures toward the sky to indicate he had come from a long way away. More murmurs came from the crowd. It was now quite obvious from their faces that they knew he was not from their world.

The brown-haired man took Billy's arm and, followed by the others, guided him up a long curved set of steps to an enormous platform built at the very top of what must have been the tallest tree on the island. There was a clear view in all directions and Billy knew this had to be a lookout tower of some kind. Wooden benches were scattered around and everyone took a seat. The man named Yan indicated to Billy that he would like to know more about what he was doing here.

Billy pointed to the sky, then to the far mountains and began to trace them in the air with his hands. With his forefinger he drew a curving line down the slope of his imaginary mountains to the floor of the platform. By wiggling his fingers he tried to convey the idea of the ocean shore and the road going under it. Everyone seemed to understand.

Getting across the idea of the kidnapping was going to be more difficult. Billy retraced the mountain roadway with his finger and then moved into a crouching position with his hands on a make-believe steering wheel. Yan was becoming intensely curious.

Now came the trickiest part of all.

After some thought Billy wandered through the crowd, picked a boy about his own age and brought him to the centre of the floor. Placing one hand over the boy's mouth and using the other to pin both of the boy's hands behind his back, he hauled him across the platform away from his imaginary shoreline deep into his imaginary ocean.

A loud murmur broke from the crowd and Yan leaped to his feet.

It was at this point that Billy pulled the golden glove from his pocket. He had saved it till his story was finished so that its meaning would be clear. He put it on the boy's hand. Then he stepped back to see the reaction.

He might as well have lit a stick of dynamite. Yan's face froze in stark horror and the voices of the villagers exploded in a deafening roar. Billy had prayed the golden glove would hold some meaning for someone, but he had never dreamed of this reaction.

The ringing cries continued as the crowd crushed in tightly around Yan, who reached out with a trembling hand to take the glove and clutched it to his chest as though it were the most precious thing in the world. Billy would have given anything to be able to speak Yan's language and learn the identity of the boy with the red hair.

The sense of outrage that swept the lookout platform did not last for long. Yan immediately took command and the look on his face changed to one of urgency. He consulted briefly with four older men and in less than a minute they were all nodding in agreement. Then, before Billy could catch his breath, Yan took him by the arm and rushed him back down the curving staircase and along a series of boughs and bridges to a platform similar to the one on which he had landed earlier. Only this time there were dozens of giant birds perched in the surrounding trees.

Yan whistled sharply twice and two of the creatures slipped from their boughs and glided soundlessly down to the platform. As before, they were already saddled and ready to take flight.

Suddenly Billy found himself being lifted up and placed on one of the birds. Yan clasped his shoulder briefly, smiled reassuringly and then mounted another bird himself. He spoke hurriedly to one of the women and shouted to the other villagers behind her. Their excitement was noisy and full of urgency.

As the crowd gathered, shouting and waving, the two giant hawks took flight.

* * *

The flight out over the swamp was swift and had none of the leisurely swoops Billy had enjoyed on his way in to the jungle island. Wherever they were heading, it obviously had to do with the identity of the kidnapped boy. He certainly had to be well known and very important to be causing so much excitement.

It was possible that Yan knew the boy's parents and perhaps *they* would know where to find the man in black. At any rate there was no other hope that Billy might be able to regain his canteen of precious fluid and find some way to fly back home to Nightcross.

The thought of his mom and dad sitting beside their applewood fire, his dad snoozing in his chair, his mom reading the paper, gave Billy a lump in his throat. Boy, what a story he would have to tell them when he got home! Then he thought of Alan and Jerry and wondered if there were search parties looking for him in the woods beyond town. Maybe his picture was even in the town newspaper?

Vast tracts of green forest appeared below, broken only by rivers and large blue lakes. Then rolling sand dunes slid beneath. Ahead, the rim of mountains, once fuzzy shadows on the horizon, grew larger and better defined as they slowly came into focus. Billy constantly marvelled at how far he could see—a lot farther than back home, even in an airplane. It was as though there were no real horizons here, but of course that was absurd.

When the mountains were very close Billy called out to Yan, who pointed toward a narrow cleft in the granite wall that Billy hadn't seen. Soon the great hawks and their passengers were sailing right into the cleft, which turned out to be a narrow chasm of black rock whose walls were frighteningly close, offering little more room than the wingspan of the birds.

Bend after bend the chasm twisted, turned and climbed its tortuous way through the broad range of mountains. Every so often Yan would give a little wave to indicate there was nothing to fear and that all was proceeding well. How Billy wished he could talk to this man! Perhaps where they were going there would be someone who could teach him Yan's language.

A little later the tree man called out something that sounded like *Vensor* and pointed toward the next bend. Billy strained forward on his hawk to get a better view.

As they rounded the last curve an awesome sight swept into view. An enormous city built into the side of a snow-white mountain sparkled in the light of the cloudless sky. To Billy's astonished eyes it seemed to be made of blue crystal. Sharp-angled rooftops, domes and spires rose in many levels up the slope of the mountain. Above the streets transparent, tubular walkways connected some of the taller structures and people glided through them on moving sidewalks.

The whole look of Vensor reminded Billy of a dream he had had when he was very young, in which he had travelled into the far future. But this was no earthly future, he was convinced of that! The architecture was too strange for any building on his own planet, too delicate and complex. He couldn't even think of the right words to describe it.

At the top of the city, higher than the other structures and dominated by a cluster of pale blue towers, stood a castle. Waving for Billy to follow, Yan swooped down towards it.

7

The City of Vensor

Billy was not long in discovering the identity of the boy with the red hair. The moment he looked into the face of the King (whose name Yan taught him to pronounce as *Farron*) and saw the sadness in his eyes, he knew the boy must be his son.

They met in a large, crystal-walled room hung with queer tapestries whose colours kept melding together. As Yan's version of the kidnapping unfolded, King Farron listened intently, his hands constantly caressing the golden glove that lay in his lap. It was obvious to Billy as he watched them that Yan, too, was an important man in the kingdom — perhaps even a Prince.

Finally, at the end of Yan's tale, the King gestured to Billy to speak. He appeared as fascinated as the woodsmen had been—and even occasionally as amused — by the sounds that came out of the boy's mouth.

After further discussion with Yan, Farron summoned someone else to listen to Billy's speech—an elderly gentleman who was wearing an elaborate coat with huge sleeves. He looked rather comical because his head was much too large for his tall, thin body and he moved in a kind of shuffling dance as he crossed the floor. Even so, he listened very carefully to the boy, his ancient face alert and his eyes twinkling as Billy tried to make him understand.

It was clear that the man was a teacher or scientist from the way he encouraged Billy to stop, start, pause and repeat himself, all with deft motions of his fingers. Afterward the King issued instructions and the old man bowed as he took his leave. But on his way out he reached down behind Billy's ear and with a broad flourish produced a large cookie which he promptly handed to the boy. Yan laughed and the King's sad face wrinkled into a smile. Billy was too surprised to do anything but stare vacantly at the departing figure. The old man was *more* than a scientist or teacher. He was also a magician!

When he had gone the smile faded from the King's face and he shook his head gravely. After pacing up and down in silence for some time he stopped abruptly, clapped the golden glove in the open palm of his left hand, and putting his arms over their shoulders, led Yan and Billy out of the room. They went down a winding staircase to a lower floor and into a chamber that was covered from floor to ceiling with maps. The King stopped in front of one of the panels and invited Yan and Billy to look.

What Billy saw was a drawing of an ocean bed with circles and numbers that didn't mean anything to him. Along the top, however, the map showed part of a shoreline with mountains and a green line that curved and twisted in a way that seemed familiar. Of course! That was the mountain road and right *there* was the spot where the young prince had been handed over to the men from the sea!

As though reading his young visitor's mind King Farron tapped his finger where the road entered the ocean and began to draw it down over the surface of the map following a faint string of dots. No doubt about it, this was the undersea road which the second ski-car had used to carry away the Prince. Billy watched in suspense as the King traced its path over the seabed.

His finger came to a small square which, judging by the colour contours of the map, was at the deepest part of the ocean. The King tapped again, but this time with a note of finality. "*Mordra!*" he cried in a hoarse whisper.

Yan nodded gloomily and noticed the puzzled expression on Billy's face. He said something to an attendant who brought in a large, flat folder. It contained a series of pictures which Yan handed over for Billy's inspection.

He had never seen anything like them before. At first he couldn't make out what the strangely luminous brown and green images represented. It was like peering through the misty depths of the ocean. Of course, that was it... Mordra! The city at the bottom of the sea!

Billy stared at tall buildings and connecting passageways glowing with an eerie light. He shuddered. What a spooky place! It looked dark and evil and reminded him of a city he had created in his imagination one wet Saturday while playing with the family aquarium. He had put his miniature submarine into the tank to attack the city, but he had got into trouble when it had terrified the fish.

He examined each picture carefully, intrigued by the eye-shaped windows and wondering what kind of people lived behind them. As he handed the pictures back to the King there were a dozen questions on his lips, but no way of asking them.

King Farron must have understood his state of mind because there was no doubt as to what the next panel he stopped at represented. It was a map of his kingdom, the kingdom of *Zomara,* as Farron pronounced it.

Here, surrounded by ocean, was an enormous island covered entirely by mountains except for several large pockets of flat land. At the lower left was the place where the road ran into the sea. Following it inland, Billy found the tunnel through the mountains leading to the jungle where he had escaped from the tall man. Yan pointed out his tree village, then guided Billy's eyes over the blue lakes and brown deserts to the mountains where the city of Vensor was perched at the end of a long chasm.

The other flat areas intrigued Billy and he pointed to them. They were located at the extreme ends of the island, but were all connected by road to Yan's valley and thus to Vensor. Each was marked in a different colour: one was golden, one almost black, and the farthest, which was the most interesting, was a colour Billy would know anywhere—the strange light blue of the fantastic bubble that had brought him here.

The King smiled. He touched his own lips, then Billy's, to suggest that answers would have to wait until they could understand each other.

But Billy could not wait. His mind was bursting with even more important questions, and although no one could understand him, he had to ask them. Despite a gentle reminder from Yan that he was, after all, in the presence of a King and must not let his emotions get the better of him, he moved his arms beyond the borders of the map and looked imploringly at Farron.

The King nodded graciously and pointed to a larger map on the opposite side of the room. Billy ran over to it and saw that the familiar blue ocean was now greatly expanded and contained no less than five islands, including Zomara. Beyond the ocean, running all the way around the borders of the huge map, was a ring of mountains. Beyond these mountains was—nothing!

Just when Billy thought he had solved one mystery another loomed before him. Again he turned to the King and again he extended his arms beyond the borders of the map. Farron looked at Yan and chuckled, then pointed to the far end of the room where an even larger map was hanging. This one was all black except for thousands of tiny white dots and clusters of dots. Someone else might have wondered what they were, but not Billy. It was a map of the universe, the kind of star chart he often spent hours poring over as he worked with his telescope.

Running up to it Billy stared long and hard, his eyes desperately searching for those familiar patterns or constellations he could recognize in the Nightcross sky. But they weren't there!

King Farron and Yan sensed Billy's distress. This time it was Yan who helped him. He touched a cluster of white dots near the centre of the map. It consisted of a large bright dot with four smaller ones circling it. The Prince touched one of the four and Billy knew this was the planet he was standing on. It was one of four planets with a sun at the centre, not unlike the Solar System, but definitely not *the* Solar System.

Suddenly it was all too much to comprehend and Billy had to sit down. Dazed, he sipped at the drink and nibbled at the cookies that were brought to him.

Where had the black hole taken him? Where in the universe was he? Worse still . . . in *what* universe was he?

King Farron directed Billy's attention toward the map flanking the one he was looking at. It was an enlargement of the star system Yan had just indicated, the one they were part of.

Three of the planets were spheres like the Earth or Mars or Venus and quite normal looking. But the fourth was queer. His science teacher's eyes would have popped if he had been with Billy at this moment. It went against all the laws of physics and made no sense whatever. Billy hoped it wouldn't be the planet the King would finally point to, but it was!

The planet of Zomar was shaped the way many people believed the Earth to be before Christopher Columbus proved otherwise. If you travelled far enough in any direction you wouldn't come back to where you started—you would simply fall off!

The planet was flat as a pancake!

* * *

Over the next two or three days King Farron saw to
it that Billy was kept busy, too busy in fact to dwell
on the queer features of a planet that did not fit in
with anything he had ever learned in science class.

Or was it four or five days—or only one day—that
he was kept so busy? Where there were no clocks,
where the sun never set and where nobody ever
seemed to sleep or sit down to eat a decent meal,
there was no way of telling how much time had
gone by. Or even if any time had gone by at all!

The King was determined that Billy should learn
the language of Zomara, so he placed him under the
care of the elderly magician, Azidor, who turned out
to be the King's chief scientist. The lessons took
place in a huge laboratory deep in the basement of
the castle. Billy was amazed by the odd-looking
equipment and the rows and rows of crystals, but he
was even more surprised by the unusual teaching
method.

Azidor got Billy to examine pictures of hundreds
of different objects and to describe in his own language what he thought they were—objects like doors
and windows and shoes, as well as many things he

could not recognize but only guess at. And all the while Azidor would put different blocks of crystals on the table in front of him, watch their colours change and make notes. Every few minutes he would consult a large wall panel of crystals, which looked like the inside of a beehive with different coloured pencils sticking out, and change the positions of the "pencils."

Most peculiar! But no more peculiar than Azidor himself. Billy found he couldn't take his eyes off this bulb-headed man who worked with the crystals as though they were tinker toys, who danced everywhere he moved in the lab and who produced teapots and cups just by clapping his hands together— not to mention fruit and cookies out of Billy's ears, nose and jacket collar with no more than the snap of his fingers.

The voice experiments lasted through many sessions, during which time Billy never left the laboratory. Then at one of their meetings Azidor put a necklace of tiny, multi-coloured crystals around his neck and allowed him to venture out to explore the streets and buildings of the city.

The sights were marvellous and Billy kept describing them out loud just in case the necklace was supposed to pick up his voice. But what gave him the most pleasure was not the city so much as the companion he was provided with.

He had caught glimpses of her down corridors and in rooms several times before, but had not actually met her until now. She was the Princess Elanna, King Farron's daughter and the sister of the missing Prince, whose name Billy discovered was Ladrion. She was about Billy's age, with sparkling blue eyes and a happy smile—and she was as much fun to be with (though Billy found this hard to admit at first) as Alan or Jerry back home. Neither could understand what the other was saying, of course, but oddly enough this didn't seem to matter on that marvellous first outing in the city.

It was the fact that Elanna liked *doing* things that excited Billy—like riding the glass elevators and walkways of the towers, or playing hide-and-seek in the ancient ruins of the older part of the city, with their nooks and crannies and beams to tightrope along.

Most fun of all was a toboggan track in the centre of a long, narrow park that ran all the way down through the city, curving under bridges and culverts and around great stone walls. The run was breathtaking! Elanna held on tightly to Billy as they zoomed and dipped. Twice the toboggan actually took off from the top of sharp knolls and glided through the air for a short distance. By the end they were so excited and dizzy that they couldn't walk without tumbling over like clowns in a circus.

There were several outings like this, but the one that impressed Billy the most was a trip to the Zomar Museum, a huge crystal building where they saw an exhibit of the most amazingly life-like figures. King Farron was there looking imperial and handsome, and beside him Elanna's mother, Lusarra. She was very lovely, but from the sadness in the Princess's eyes Billy gathered she was no longer alive.

It was not until later, when Billy and Elanna could communicate in words, that he learned that Lusarra had been an explorer—a legend, in fact, throughout all the kingdoms of Zomar. Some years before she had set out with an expedition to penetrate the mountain ranges encircling the flat planet in order to be the first to see and stand on the extreme outer edge. The expedition had never returned and all attempts to find it had failed. Billy could not help noticing that Elanna's face bore a striking resemblance to her mother's.

There were figures that Billy assumed to be Elanna's grandparents and great-grandparents as well as many other important looking people the Princess had no way of identifying for her new friend. There were also depictions of battles that had been fought in the distant past between the different island kingdoms of Zomar—each set against a vivid dramatic backdrop.

The very last exhibit had a strange hypnotic effect on Billy. It was set off in a corner, isolated from the others. Elanna, for some reason, did not want to linger in front of it. She tugged impatiently at Billy's arm, but he couldn't take his eyes off the figure in the large glass case.

It was the figure of a woman with a hauntingly beautiful face, a face so well moulded that it seemed alive. Billy was spellbound by the burning green eyes and the dark red lips poised ready to speak. She wore a golden crown and was richly dressed in royal robes. Was she a queen of one of the other island kingdoms of Zomar—perhaps even a relative of King Farron himself?

But if this were so, why was she kept apart from the others?

Even more puzzling was the fact that the figure stood in a glass case filled with pale blue water. Sea grass waved gently from rocky clefts strewn with clam shells, and queer, flat-headed fish flitted this way and that around the royal figure. What, Billy marvelled, would a queen be doing at the bottom of the sea?

As he stared into the glass case he became aware that in the inky gloom behind the queen there were paintings that seemed almost real. But they were indistinct and continually changing.

Suddenly he realized he was looking at the ramparts and towers of an enormous city.

The lighted windows twinkling in the ocean gloom struck a strong chord of recognition. "Mordra!" he whispered hoarsely, much the way King Farron had done when he had shown him the pictures of the city at the bottom of the sea. "She must be the Queen of Mordra, the one who had Prince Ladrion kidnapped!"

"Mordra!" Elanna repeated, nodding darkly.

8
The Black Earrings

At the end of each outing Elanna and Billy would report to Azidor who would spend long periods checking the instruments on his beehive panel. Occasionally he would ask Billy to say something and then alter the arrangement of the crystals in the necklace. After these sessions he would always perform a trick or two for his young friends before sending them off to play somewhere in the castle.

Although Billy and Elanna spent a lot of time together they had to communicate by acting out since, apart from their names and a few other sounds, they still had no spoken language to share. Sometimes Billy would entertain Elanna by drawing pictures of his family and friends, his house in Nightcross, cars and airplanes and animals—and the strange magical bubble that had carried him through the black hole to Zomar. At other times Elanna would show Billy pictures of the curious sights in the five kingdoms of Zomar.

One day—Billy still couldn't get out of the habit of thinking in days even though there weren't any—Azidor greeted the two children with an enormous smile. He was vigorously rubbing his hands together the way Billy's dad always did when about to spring a big surprise. He put his finger to his lips to indicate absolute silence, then produced three small, flat, green boxes. He gave one to each and kept one for himself.

Billy and Elanna exchanged excited glances as they opened their gifts. Inside each box was a pair of small, black, crystal earrings. Still keeping his finger to his lips Azidor motioned to the children to put them on. He clamped a pair of crystals on his own ears, smiled broadly at Billy and then spoke: *"Sor vara lit Zomar cul men Zomara, Beellee!"*

But that wasn't what Billy heard, not with the strange crystal earrings. What sounded in his ears was, "Welcome to the Kingdom of Zomara, Billy, on the planet of Zomar!"

Billy jumped up into the air yelling *"Zowee!"* He grabbed the ancient scientist's hand and shouted, "Am I ever glad to know you, Azidor!"

And Azidor and Elanna heard *"Yor grenada, Azidor!"*

Now it was their turn to jump for joy. They clasped Billy's hands and danced around the laboratory, laughing as though at a birthday party.

"Oh, Billy," said Elanna over and over, "we'll have such fun talking! We have so much to tell each other!"

What a miracle! Billy thought. What marvellous crystals! They could make any language sound just like your own! How great they would be back on Earth!

Azidor served tea and cookies and he and his two companions chatted just for the sake of chatting.

"Believe it or not, Billy, I have been working on this invention for more than half a lifetime," the aged scientist said at last. "We speak several different languages here on Zomar, just as you probably do where you come from, and I have always believed that the crystals held the secret of enabling people to understand each other." The old man's eyes were filled with tears of joy. "At last we have discovered that they do."

"I have so many questions to ask you, Azidor and"—Billy's face reddened slightly—"and you too, Elanna."

The Princess smiled back in sheer delight.

"And we, you!" replied the scientist. "But we shall have to proceed in some kind of order. First, of course, King Farron must be told of our good fortune. He and Prince Yan from the Tree Country have a great deal to discuss with you."

"And I have to find out how to get back home to

Mom and Dad," added Billy softly.

"Of course you do." Azidor smiled. "And we shall help you. But that will come later. First we must see His Majesty."

The scientist put down his teacup and stood up. Elanna rose also, but Billy, suddenly deep in thought, remained in his chair.

"You have a question, Billy, before we go?" asked the old man.

Billy nodded briskly. "Why do you call your planet Zomar?"

"Because Zomar was the name of one of two brothers—both space explorers—who first discovered this planet," replied Azidor. "Astron was his brother's name. Both good names, don't you think?"

"Oh, yes, they are," replied Billy, "but—but— *space explorers?*"

Elanna laughed. "I tried to explain that to you in the museum, Billy, but of course you couldn't understand what I was saying."

"Were they both in the exhibit?"

"They were, and you nudged me and smiled to show you liked them."

"Gosh!"

"Zomar and Astron," continued Azidor, "fled with their people from a dying planet. Their fleet landed on this planet to refuel and replenish their food and water supplies before proceeding. Their goal was a distant star system where they planned to start a new life. But while here Astron, who I am proud to say was an ancestor of mine, discovered the unique substance that abounds on this planet and that still bears his name."

"Astron?"

"That's right. And because of it the space travellers never left. They settled down and"—he waved his arms majestically—"here we all are." He patted Elanna's golden hair with pride. "Of course there is much, much more to our history. I've given you only the barest details."

"Tell me more about the astron," asked Billy. "Why is it so special?"

"He does have a lot of questions, doesn't he, Elanna?"

"I knew he would," laughed the Princess. "This must all be so strange for him."

"Astron is found in rocks and gravel and even in our water and our air. It's a most remarkable substance altogether," continued the scientist. "It keeps our mountain homes and cities warm, it's an excellent medicine and will heal a wound in a moment. It even cooks our vegetables—that is, what few vegetables we eat."

"That's another thing," interrupted Billy. "No one ever eats around here. I haven't had a real meal since I came."

"Are you hungry?"

Billy pondered for a moment and shook his head. "No."

"Well, then, why would you want to eat?"

"We always eat back home."

"Probably because you're hungry much of the time back home," chuckled Azidor. "Here"—he gestured broadly—"the very astron in the air feeds you, nourishes you. That's why we eat very little."

"And you don't sleep either," put in Billy quickly. "I haven't had a nap yet."

"And you probably won't require one while you're here," said the old man. "Again it's the astron. It seems to take care of that problem too."

Billy was curious and persistent. "Could I see some of the stuff?"

"Some liquid astron?" Azidor reached for a test tube in a rack containing dozens of different tubes. "Of course. Here's a sample."

Billy's eyes widened in surprise at the sight of the familiar shimmering blue fluid. He took the tube from Azidor and poured a few drops on his palm. No doubt about it. This was exactly the same as the gooey contents of his canteen! No wonder the tall man had thought nothing of it. It was no more unusual than a can of oil for his dad's car.

"Astron rocks and liquid astron exist in a large quarry right here in Zomara. The rocks grow there.

We even have clusters of astronbergs on islands in different parts of the ocean. They're everywhere."

"Did you say *grow?*" asked Billy.

"Oh, yes. They are easy to spot. They're blue-white and they dissolve when they touch liquid astron. Also the volcanoes in the mountains release astron gas. Our planet wouldn't be the same without astron. It has hundreds of uses."

"How true," murmured Billy, thinking of his magical bubble. Suddenly his mind flashed back to the meteor he had found in the woods beyond Oak Street. It had been bluish-white and had melted. So that was it! The meteor had been an astronrock that had come from Zomar. It had probably exploded from a volcano and shot up into space. No wonder he had thought it looked alive. If astron could grow, then it *was* alive! And no wonder his astron bubble had carried him right up into the sky and brought him here. It had wanted to get back home as much as he did now.

So many mysteries, Billy thought, but at least I am starting to get a few answers. Still, there's a lot to learn.

"And now we must report to your father, Princess Elanna," said the old man, tapping his earrings. "He must learn of my invention."

As Azidor swept the children before him out into the passageway, Billy began bombarding his two

75

friends with further questions. "Why are there no clocks here and why don't you have any stoves or fireplaces? And why—"

Elanna burst out laughing. "What a strange world you must come from, Billy."

"I don't think it's so strange," Billy retorted. "How else could we keep warm?"

"What the Princess means," Azidor interrupted, "is that 'time' and 'fire' are unknown to us here. You'll really have to tell us about them. There's so much we want to know about your world."

"And there's something else, Azidor!" They were now almost at the map room where the King, Yan and some generals were in conference.

"What's that, Billy?"

"You don't have any wheels here! I haven't seen a single wheel since I came!"

The magician and Princess Elanna stared at each other. "Wheels?" they said together. "Whatever are they, Billy?"

9

The Bubble Commandos

The mood in the map room was tense. No ransom note or message of any kind had come from Mordra and King Farron was desperately worried about the fate of young Prince Ladrion. Something had to be done quickly or there was no telling what the "Mad Queen" would do to the boy.

Standing beside the large ocean map, addressing a group of dignitaries and people in uniform, King Farron used the term several times. So that is what they call the queen at the bottom of the sea, thought Billy, vividly remembering the exhibit. He nudged Yan, who had put on the set of black earrings Azidor had given him when they first entered the room.

"She's the King's sister, Billy," he whispered. "She's mad. Quite mad. She hates the King and has sworn revenge on him."

"Why?" whispered Billy.

"Because he banished her from Zomara—after the uprising."

"Uprising?"

"Shhh! We can't talk now," Yan whispered. "She tried to take the country away from the King— wanted to make slaves of us all—so he banished her. I'll tell you more later."

Billy was not to be hushed. "How mad is she?"

Yan put a gloved hand to the boy's lips. "Madder than you can imagine," he whispered. "She has to be kept in a cage most of the time. Sometimes she seems normal, but never for long. Most of the time she screams and yells and waves her arms and dances. She's carried in a golden cage wherever she goes. Even her throne is in a cage."

A loud *Shhh* came from Azidor who was straining his ears to hear King Farron's concluding remarks.

"And that just about sums it up," said the King, pointing once more to the square on the map that represented the city at the bottom of the sea. "The situation is not only desperate, it seems impossible. The only way for Prince Yan and his commando team to reach Mordra is by ski-car along the under-sea highway, but the Queen's crystal detectors will warn her of their coming long before they get there. If we could approach the city from some other direction we might have a chance, but there is no other way—the city is too deep.

"There must be a solution to the problem, but after hours of discussion we seem to be no nearer to it. We've even had the benefit of Prince Yan from the Tree Country and"—here he glanced briefly in Billy's direction—"our most welcome young friend from beyond the sky who gave us the vital link in our search for Prince Ladrion. But we still seem to be getting nowhere."

King Farron stopped then, with a catch in his voice that brought tears to the eyes of many, and sat down. Billy had never seen a face that looked so haggard and forlorn. A heavy silence settled upon the room.

Suddenly a thought struck Billy that seemed so obvious he wondered why no one had suggested it. "Why not use submarines?" he blurted out.

The King looked up, not understanding what Billy was saying. Quickly Azidor attached a set of earrings to his ears. Billy repeated his question and the King marvelled at the miracle of the earrings, smiling warmly at the old scientist.

"Submarines?" Farron asked after a pause. "We know nothing of submarines. What are they, Billy?"

Billy went to the front of the map room while the wizard distributed earrings to the military people. He explained as best he could, even drawing pictures on a large sheet of paper, but the idea of a submarine seemed too difficult to grasp for people who had never known propellers or wheels.

"Very good, Billy," applauded the King. "We do have boats, but we have no way of making them go under water."

"Ski-cars go under water," Billy replied.

"The ski-car can never be more than a whisker above the road bed. It glides on magnetic waves," said the King.

"The steering stick changes the angles of the magnetic plates on the bottom of the car," added Azidor. "That's what controls its speed and direction. With your help, Billy, I can see the possibility of building a submarine, but it would not be soon enough to rescue Prince Ladrion."

There was a low murmur of voices that subsided as King Farron motioned for silence.

Then Princess Elanna was on her feet. "Billy, do you remember the picture you once drew to show me how you got here? The drawing of the bubble? You never told me how you made it. Could the bubble help us to rescue Ladrion? Can you make one?"

Her face held such a pleading look that Billy could not refuse. He thought for a long moment, then nodded. Yes, it was time to reveal the secret of the bubble. He had held back from telling anyone, even Azidor and Elanna, because of his terrible experience with the tall man with the narrow face.

But only friends were here. And besides, he didn't need his canteen anymore. He could get all the astron he would ever need.

Billy turned toward the King. "I have something to show you, sir, but I don't know if it'll work in water."

"What is it, Billy?"

"Could I have some goo, sir?"

"Some what?"

"Some liquid astron."

The King looked puzzled and glanced toward Azidor. The scientist shrugged and clapped his hands. A servant left the room and returned a moment later with a glass of the blue fluid.

"It's what I had in my canteen before the tall man stole it," Billy said as he took his brother's plastic loop from his pocket and dipped it into the fluid.

Yan chuckled from the audience and said, "Is this some kind of toy, Billy?"

Billy grinned, then blew into the loop. Princess Elanna gasped and everyone sat forward, openmouthed, staring at the shimmering apparition before them.

"Now watch!" said Billy, making a sudden jump and landing squarely inside the hovering globe.

The King got to his feet, shaking visibly. "I do not believe it! I do not believe what I see!"

"This is no trick," Billy assured him. "It's done with your own astron. Watch this!" He sailed over the heads of the bewildered audience and did a couple of circles around the room before landing once more in front of the King.

"Would you like to try it, sir?" Billy asked, but the King didn't quite know what to say.

"Let me try it, Billy!" exclaimed the Princess.

A moment later she was airborne, laughing gaily as she repeated Billy's movements.

King Farron mopped his brow with his sleeve, causing his crown to slip back and making him look rather comical. "This is remarkable, Billy, remarkable!" He wrung his hands together and said to Azidor, "What do you think? Will it stand the water pressure?"

"Why not try it out, Your Majesty?"

The King nodded. "Come along, Billy."

Down the corridor they went, led by King Farron and Azidor. Moments later they were all standing around the monarch's private swimming pool.

"All right," called the King, "let's see if it works. Go ahead, lad!"

Billy had floated along the passageway in the bubble. He now glided off the edge of the pool and plunged down toward the surface of the water. It worked perfectly. Not the slightest strain was evident on the walls of the bubble as it sank to the bottom.

A thunderous roar of approval echoed in Billy's ears as the bubble emerged and he alighted in a shower of drops in front of the King. The experiment was a total success.

*   *   *

In view of the extreme urgency of the situation, preparations for the departure of Yan and his bubble commandos proceeded at a frantic pace. Billy quickly trained the soldiers in the use of his plastic loop and then showed them how to deflate the bubbles with a drop of liquid astron. It was essential that none be left behind for the Mordrians to use.

But despite his help, Billy was in for a great disappointment. The King absolutely refused to allow him and Elanna to go with Yan to Mordra. They were both children, he said, and that was the end of it. Furthermore, Farron would not let them sulk over the decision. For the sake of the morale of Yan and the sixteen men and women in his commando team they had to accept his word in good spirits.

Then came zero hour.

Everyone gathered on the flat-topped tower which was the secret launching base for the expedition. Azidor supplied each commando with a canteen of astron and a wire loop, and King Farron wished them well on the dangerous mission that lay ahead.

The King then looked at Billy and smiled briefly. "In view of the vital assistance he has given us," he announced, "I have decided to allow Billy the honour of giving the final orders to the soldiers and the royal command to depart."

The boy's face beamed. "Do you really mean that, sir?"

"Of course I do, Billy. If it had not been for you we would still be trying to find a way to get to Mordra."

"Thank you, sir! Thank you!"

Billy took up his position in front of Yan and the soldiers. Everyone expected him to give the command to take up the loops and blow the bubbles, but Billy had a different idea. Quick as a flash he dipped his plastic loop into the canteen of liquid astron Azidor had given him, withdrew it and blew long and hard.

Before everyone's astonished eyes a whole string of giant bubbles shot away from the loop and hovered just in front of the soldiers.

"Enter your bubbles!" commanded Billy in a voice that made up in volume what it lacked in authority. Briskly and professionally the commandos entered the bubbles and seconds later were poised above the roof, ready for take-off.

"In the name of the King, depart!" shouted Billy.

"And life be with you!" added Farron solemnly. "Bring my boy back to me!"

"*Gro mado bellor!*" chanted Azidor, opening his arms as though in blessing. "*Gro mado bellor!*" he repeated—ancient and holy words that would not convert themselves into English in Billy's earrings.

Yan's bubble rose up from the rooftop and launched out over the edge. The others followed suit. Within seconds they had disappeared into the blue Zomarian sky.

10

The Flight to Mordra

That afternoon—or it could have been morning or night—Billy and Elanna visited the Vensor Observatory located on a mountain peak a short distance from the city. Their spirits had dropped following the departure of Yan as they realized that Prince Ladrion's fate was now entirely out of their hands. All they could do was wait, and already that strange emptiness that goes with waiting was weighing heavily on them.

They passed exhibit after exhibit containing exquisite models of the Zomar solar system as well as neighbouring star systems, but there was none of the excitement that Billy would normally have felt nor any of the enthusiasm Elanna would usually have shown as these wonders were revealed. Somehow all life and spirit had gone out of their fun.

"It's not fair that Father wouldn't let us go with Yan," grumbled Elanna after a long silence.

"I know," sighed Billy. "I know."

And a little later, "We wouldn't have been a nuisance. We would have been a lot of help."

"You're right. And it wouldn't have been dangerous, really. Not for us."

"I know."

They were walking down a long glass ramp toward an exhibit that just might have jarred Billy back to his usual cheerful self—the original space craft, preserved in every detail, that had brought Zomar and Astron to this planet—when the sudden crackle of a voice from a loudspeaker stopped them in their tracks:

Princess Elanna and Master Billy Brown, report to Chief Scientist Azidor immediately! It is urgent! Report to Azidor immediately!

"I wonder what that means?" said Elanna.

"I don't know, but let's hurry and find out!" exclaimed Billy, a glint of adventure suddenly returning to his eyes.

When they burst into his laboratory Azidor was standing by a table repeatedly dipping a wire loop into a beaker of astron and raising it to his lips and blowing.

But nothing was happening!

"This is terrible! Terrible!" he was muttering between puffs of breath.

"What is it?" asked Billy, not quite grasping the problem.

"No bubbles! No bubbles! Nothing! I can't understand it. What has gone wrong? That's why I called you, to tell me what went wrong. I can't make any bubbles!"

Quickly Billy took his loop from his pocket, dipped it into the shimmering liquid and blew. A beautiful blue bubble suddenly appeared.

"See!" he protested. "There's nothing wrong, Azidor. It works fine."

"What—what—" stammered the ancient scientist, repeating Billy's action.

But once again nothing happened.

"I can't understand it," said Billy. "It works when I do it."

"This doesn't make sense," exclaimed Elanna.

"Very, very peculiar," whispered the scientist.

The three of them stood staring at the pale blue contents of the beaker, their brows wrinkled in puzzlement.

It was Elanna who broke the silence. She glanced from Billy's loop to the magician's with a quizzical expression.

"Billy, your loop is different from Azidor's!"

Billy shook his head. "They amount to the same thing, Elanna. We use both kinds back home. Azidor said that plastic can't be made on Zomar, so I told him to use wire. There's no difference."

"Oh," said the Princess, "I just thought that—"

"Wait! Wait!" cried the old scientist, clutching

Billy's arm. "Maybe there is a difference! Maybe you've hit on something, Elanna. Here, Billy, let's exchange loops."

Billy handed his plastic loop to Azidor and took the wire one.

"Now," breathed the wizard, his eyes narrowing mysteriously, "let's see what happens." He dipped the plastic loop, and as he blew, the familiar bubble expanded into view. "Your turn, my boy!"

Billy followed, using Azidor's wire loop, but dip and puff though he might, nothing happened. He was frustrated and amazed. "I can't understand it."

"I can!" proclaimed Azidor, prancing around the room and waving the plastic loop before the eyes of the two children. "Don't you see, Billy? It only works when you use a plastic loop. There must be some special reaction that occurs when liquid astron comes into contact with plastic. That's the magic, Billy! That's why you have your magic bubbles! The astron doesn't work with wire!"

Billy's eyes widened in amazement. "If I had picked up one of my brother's wire loops instead of this plastic one, then—then—"

"Then," put in Elanna, "there would have been no bubble and you would never have found us! It's all very strange, isn't it, Billy?"

Azidor had begun to bob his bulbous head in agreement when suddenly he went rigid with horror.

"Oh—oh, my goodness!" he gasped, whirling toward the door. "This is awful! Awful! I knew I should have tested those loops before take-off. I knew it! But we were in such a rush. This is awful! I must see His Majesty right away. Not a moment to lose!"

"What is it?" yelled Billy and Elanna at the same time, not understanding the reason for the rush.

"Don't you see? Don't you see?" howled the old man as he disappeared from view, his voice trailing down the hall. "Yan and his bubble squad won't be able to get back! They won't be able to escape from Mordra! They're counting on fresh bubbles—that's part of the escape plan! But they have wire loops. They won't be able to make any fresh bubbles!"

Billy and Elanna rushed out into the corridor, but the wizard had already vanished up the staircase.

* * *

As it turned out, the King had no decision to make regarding the grave problem that had arisen. Elanna and Billy acted without delay. They packed the few vital items they knew they would have to take and in one large bubble they set off from a balcony high up on the castle wall.

By the time King Farron read with startled, unbelieving eyes the note his daughter had left for him they were well on their way.

"Those children! Those stubborn, foolhardy children!" he groaned over and over as he paced the tower roof. Peering into the blue beyond, he could see nothing but snow and rock and a thread of water coursing down the mountainside.

"You mean those brave children, Your Majesty," corrected Azidor, his concern visible only in the clasping and unclasping of his long fingers.

"Whatever am I to do?"

"There's nothing you can do. Billy has the plastic loop. He and Elanna will try to intercept Yan and his team in the astron quarries near Mordra before they attempt to enter the undersea city. There's nothing we can do but wait."

"Oh, dear, oh, dear . . . " The King's voice fell into silence.

"*Gro mado bellor!*" intoned the wizard, his face turned to the abyss into which Billy and Elanna had disappeared. "*Gro mado bellor!*"

In the bubbleship Elanna turned from gazing at the craggy walls of the chasm flashing by and gave Billy's hand a squeeze. "That was a nice start, Billy. Really smooth!"

Billy crossed his fingers. "I hope we finish up as well." Elanna looked at his hand and laughed out loud.

"Why did you do that?"

"What?"

"Cross your fingers."

"Oh, I don't know. Grandma always does it. She says it brings good luck."

"Does it work?"

Billy shrugged. "Who knows? I've never really thought about it. I've just always done it."

Elanna pursed her lips in a determined way and crossed the fingers on both her hands. "Now it has to work, Billy!"

He looked away from her and his smile grew serious. "I sure hope your father won't be too upset. You really should have stayed behind."

The Princess shook her head. "He knows I'd never let you go without me."

"But it's even worse than that, Elanna. If I hadn't been such a show-off on top of the tower all this wouldn't have happened. We'd have discovered that the wire loops don't work and I could have given my plastic one to Yan." Billy slouched against the wall of their bubble and toyed with a button on his suede jacket.

Elanna put her hand on his arm. "Don't blame yourself, Billy", she said softly. "You did what you thought was right at the time. You didn't know about the wire not working. And besides"—the Princess's face lit with a mischievous grin—"we wouldn't be having this adventure if you hadn't blown all those bubbles yourself."

Before long the opening of the chasm swept into view. Ahead loomed brown sand dunes, beyond which lay the great forest, the swamp and the far mountains.

"We'll be turning left here," said Elanna, indicating on her map their planned route across Zomara.

"We'll be crossing over one of the other big valleys then?"

"We will. You'll see the quarries where the magno-slates come from."

Soon the chasm was far behind and they were racing down a broad pass in the mountains. The land below was all dark rock with traces of snow and a sparkling blue river running down the centre.

Then they took another turn and beneath them stretched a valley very different from any Billy had yet seen. He thought he could be looking down at the surface of the moon, except that there were strange white gashes where quarries had bitten into the craters. From time to time they passed over clusters of homes like beads on the thread of the road and Billy watched the ski-cars speeding along like toys on a track.

"How do they cut the rocks into plates for the ski-cars?" he asked.

"They use a special crystal," Elanna answered.

"It has a ray that will cut through almost anything. Yan took one along in his pouch in case it is needed."

The bubbleship passed over the lip of the valley, entered another mountain pass and began heading for the ocean. Once there, the two adventurers would be on the final lap of their journey to the city of Mordra. Beyond the end of the pass they could already see the first glimmerings of water.

"We're making excellent progress," Elanna commented. "We should be at Mordra before the fourth bleep."

Billy looked questioningly at her.

"I mean when my pocket crystal goes bleep," said Elanna, "for the fourth time. It has already bleeped twice. So we're over half way."

"Is that pocket crystal like a clock or a watch?"

"Oh, good heavens, no!" chuckled Elanna, handing the crystal to Billy. "It's not at all like the watches you've described to me."

Billy held a flat bar of smoky crystal whose surface was marked off in tiny squares. He put it to his ear, but could hear no sound coming from it.

"That crystal is co-ordinated with this," Elanna continued, producing from her pouch a map showing all the lands and oceans of Zomar. It was covered by a grid of tiny squares. "This may explain why we don't have the north, west, south or east that you've been telling us about, Billy, or the kilometres. We really don't need them. The pocket crystal lets us know where we are on Zomar whenever we want to know. It's done by coded signals. Azidor will explain it to you when we get back."

"But how can you tell how long it takes you to get somewhere?" Billy asked as the ocean swept into view below them.

"Oh, there you go worrying about time again," Elanna protested. "Such matters as *how long* it takes to do something don't have very much meaning here, not when we have all the time in the world to begin with. Time must be very precious where you come from, and distance too."

It was all very perplexing. His science teacher might have understood what Elanna was saying because he knew all about space and time, but somehow Billy doubted it.

They were both getting bored gazing down at the unchanging surface of the ocean when a fourth bleep sounded from the crystal.

"We must be directly over Mordra now," exclaimed Elanna. "Let's enter the water about... *there.*" She pointed to a stretch of ocean slightly beyond the city's location.

"This should certainly fool the Mad Queen. She'd never suspect that we would come from a direction where there are no sea roads."

Billy nodded. "It sure helps to travel by bubble when you want to fool someone."

Elanna laughed. "I'd like to see her face when Yan and father's soldiers rescue Ladrion and she finds out how we did it."

"That'll really drive her mad!" echoed Billy. With that the bubble started to dive straight down toward the milky green surface of the ocean.

11
The Astron Quarry

The bubble sped along the floor of the ocean, an iridescent sphere sliding between sea trees with bloated trunks and over waving sea grass that bobbed and bowed as it swept past. Fish as big as whales but thin as paper hovered close, their huge, flat, comic-book eyes glaring at the intruders. Below, chasms slipped away, their depths hidden in the inky blackness of the water.

"I wouldn't like to have to go down there," Elanna whispered. "No telling what you might meet."

A tremor in her voice prompted Billy to ask, "Are you afraid, Elanna?"

"Are you?"

"A little."

"Me too." She paused briefly. "I hope we get to Yan soon."

Billy gave her arm a gentle squeeze and then

pointed. "The city must be over there. Look at the light!"

A great, dome-shaped hill lay ahead, its upper edge silhouetted against a mysterious glow. At a nod from Elanna Billy made the bubble rise from the ocean floor and glide to a position just below the hill's crown where they could get a good view—but no farther. They were not taking any unnecessary risks.

Mordra was set in a broad, deep valley, its towers and spires reaching high into the ocean. Massive ramparts of green-black stone extended far out over the ocean floor. But more chilling were the thousands of oval windows twinkling with a strange green light that suggested only one thing—eyes! The eyes of someone or something that was pure evil. The eyes of a very mad Queen.

Billy motioned to Elanna and once more the bubble began to move. By the time they reached the bottom of the valley the vast black city with its thousand eyes appeared more grotesque than ever. Elanna kept close to Billy's side as they glided past its walls toward a plain of enormous slag heaps. "I hope we'll be able to catch Yan in the quarries," said Elanna, shaking her head. "I don't think I'd much like having to go in there."

"Me neither." Billy shivered.

A range of mountains loomed out of the green depths. Elanna checked her map and pointed to a roadbed which curved across the ocean floor from the city and ran up to a cave at the base of the towering slopes.

"Are those the quarries we're looking for?" asked Billy.

Elanna nodded.

There were no ski-cars on the highway, so they followed the roadbed across to the entrance. As they approached the huge metal door that sealed the mouth of the cave Billy wondered if Elanna would have to use her crystals to get it open, but the door turned out to be automatic. It slid back noiselessly, allowing the bubble to float into the dim interior, and then closed shut behind them.

"It's like some kind of watery dungeon," Billy whispered. Elanna said nothing but simply pointed toward the ceiling.

The water was beginning to lower at a quick rate, disappearing magically into the walls of the chamber which, upon closer inspection, revealed thousands upon thousands of tiny holes. When the room was empty a door ahead opened with a loud *Praanngg!* and they floated into a long, dimly lit tunnel.

In the eerie silence they landed their bubble and

Billy deflated it with a drop of astron.

"I wonder where—" he whispered, but he got no further.

Whoosh! Four tall figures were suddenly upon them, clamping hands over their mouths and scooping them up in strong arms. The children struggled vainly in the semi-darkness.

"All right, all right!" came a familiar voice at last. "Let them go!" Yan was there before them, hands planted firmly on hips, eyes wide in amazement.

"What in Zomar are you two doing here?" His voice did not have its usual friendly ring.

"We had to come, Yan!" blurted out Elanna. "You'd never have been able to return!"

"What do you mean?"

"We mean this," exclaimed Billy, holding up his plastic loop close to Yan's eyes. "Azidor discovered the wire ones don't work. Only mine works!"

"What!" Yan took his wire loop from his pocket and tested it with astron from his canteen.

"You see!" said Elanna when Yan's efforts proved useless.

"But—but—" stammered their friend, "the loops worked on the tower roof before take-off."

"Billy blew the bubbles, Yan. Don't you remember? Father gave him the honour. He used his own loop, the one he brought from home. It's made of something called plastic which Azidor says we cannot make in Zomar. The wire loops were never tested."

Yan's face brightened as he cupped Elanna's chin in one hand and ruffled Billy's hair with the other.

"So you see, we had to come," they said.

"I see." He grinned. "And you didn't by any chance have time to get permission from King Farron, did you?"

"Well—uh—" stammered Billy, looking sheepishly toward Elanna.

"Of course not." Yan sighed, shaking his head with painful slowness. "What am I going to do with you both? What am I going—"

"We'll be no trouble," protested Elanna. "We promise. We'll wait right here until you get back."

Yan frowned. He had no alternative but to agree. "Well—see that you do," he said, turning toward his team. After a brief consultation they followed him back along the main tunnel toward the entrances to a series of side passages.

Billy and Elanna walked over and sat behind a pile of recently quarried astron bricks. "Do you have tunnels like these on your planet, Billy?"

"This is just like a mine back home. I visited a coal mine one summer in British Columbia. We even went down a shaft in an elevator."

He picked up a white astron brick and began toying with it. "Why are these bricks so important to the Queen?"

"They make astron gas. All you have to do is drop them into liquid astron and they evaporate to become the very best kind of air."

Billy snapped his fingers. "They provide air for the Queen's city!"

"That's right."

He frowned. "But wait—where does the Queen get the liquid astron?"

"She's sitting on it. It's tapped from below the city."

"Ohhh!" Billy nodded with understanding, but only momentarily. A second frown furrowed his brow.

"What is it, Billy?"

"Why all the bother with underwater ski-cars and sliding doors and everything? Why didn't the Queen just build her city right against the mountain? Then she could have had all the astron bricks she wanted without fuss."

Elanna paused and a look Billy couldn't describe crossed her face. "She—*she* didn't build the city. It was someone—something—else that built Mordra. I'll tell you about it sometime."

Billy was too curious to be put off. "Tell me now, Elanna. Please. We've got time."

But the story had to wait. Yan's warning crystal began to bleep so loudly up the tunnel that they could hear it from where they were sitting.

"They're coming!" Elanna whispered, pulling Billy with her into a side tunnel.

Along the main shaft Yan's commandos were waiting in the side entrances, ice-guns drawn and held at the ready. No one moved a muscle. Everyone was waiting for the inner door of the water chamber to open and the black ski-cars to glide in.

Like a long line of beetles they came, floating in over the paved stone roadbed, dripping milky green water, their crystal headlights frosty in the gloom of the tunnel. Billy took one look and shuddered. Elanna stared, scarcely daring to breathe.

The ski-cars, each pulling a low, spacious trailer used for transporting astron bricks, halted and settled gently on the tunnel floor. Then the panel doors slid open and the occupants stepped out. From what Billy could see in the gloom they looked just like King Farron's people. They wore green coveralls and metal helmets, much like the miners he had seen in British Columbia except that their lamps were bright crystals worn on belts at their waists. They were mostly men, but there were some women among them. It seemed to Billy that all the commands were given by the women.

He had barely seconds in which to make these

observations before Yan, yelling "Shoot!" at the top of his lungs, leaped from his hiding place and began pressing the red button on his ice-gun. The miners of Mordra were caught so completely by surprise that they were literally frozen in their tracks before they could draw their weapons.

"Well done!" called Yan, reholstering his ice-gun and stepping among the immobilized figures of the Mad Queen's miners. "Pack them in that tunnel. But be careful! I don't want any arms or legs knocked off. Our quarrel is not with them."

As they were being carried away, the figures reminded Billy of the pieces in his chess set. "What will happen to them, Elanna?" he asked.

"Yan will de-ice them when he comes back for us. His ice-gun also does that."

He was relieved to hear this. The ice-gun held an awful memory for him. He could still see the bird on the skyway shattering into a hundred fragments.

A few minutes later Billy felt Yan's hand on his shoulder. The commandos, now dressed in miners' uniform, had boarded the ski-cars and were awaiting the order to advance on the underwater city. "Since you're both here," the Prince said, "there is something you can do for me. I want you to keep this." He handed Billy a green-coloured crystal the size of a pack of playing cards. "I will keep an identical one with me at all times. As long as it glows green you will know that we are all right. If it should go out, I want both of you to fly straight back to King Farron for help. Give the crystal to him. He will know what to do."

He gave Elanna a second crystal exactly like the smoky-looking one with grid lines on it. "This will get you back. You know how to use it."

The Princess nodded. A dark expression crossed Billy's face and he was about to speak, but Yan anticipated what he was going to say. "Now don't worry, either of you. I have fifteen of the finest soldiers in Zomara with me. I'll be all right." Then he smiled the warm smile Billy had seen when they first met, and put his arms around them. "Just remember to follow my orders to the letter. Don't try to become heroes or do anything foolish. We'll have Prince Ladrion back here before you can snap your fingers."

Before either could reply he had boarded the lead ski-car and closed the panel door. The long line of black machines began to move out.

12

The Green Crystal

While Billy and Elanna awaited the return of Prince Yan they decided they could at least be comfortable. One of the ski-cars had not been used, so they climbed inside and sat down on the well-padded leather seats. Billy placed the crystal on a small shelf in front of them where it glowed green in the semi-darkness.

"Are you okay?" he asked after a long silence.

Elanna nodded, whispering, "It's exciting, isn't it?"

Billy pursed his lips. "Uh-huh!"

The Princess picked up the crystal and Billy studied the green glow on her face. "It makes you look spooky," he said.

She held it close to Billy's nose and laughed at the effect. "You too."

Billy turned around in his seat and scanned the interior of the car. Memories of the tall man came to him and made him shiver. He decided he did not like to think about things like that and said, "Tell me the story you promised about who built the underwater city."

Elanna shook her head. "You wouldn't want to hear that now. Later, Billy, when we get back home."

But he was not to be put off. Besides, he knew they would probably have a long wait before Yan returned. "No, I want to hear it now. It sounds interesting." He toyed with the green crystal. "We have nothing else to do."

"It's kind of creepy."

"That's all right."

She sighed and straightened her tunic. "Well, if you insist," she said. Billy folded his arms and leaned back in his seat.

"Long after Astron and Zomar colonized this planet some other people came to Zomar in large ships from somewhere out in space. One of their ships is still kept in Vensor and I'll take you to see it when we get home. The odd thing about those ships was that they were full of water."

"What?" said Billy, leaning forward.

"That's right, water. The people in them had come from a planet that was completely covered by a great sea. They were fish people and could only live or travel under water."

Billy whistled. "Fish people! Wow!"

"No one knows why they came here, but we do know they didn't have enough fuel to leave. Anyway, they soon discovered that liquid astron was all the food they needed, so they built the city of Mordra on the spot where astron bubbles up from the ocean bottom." She paused and her face darkened in the gloomy light. "There was another reason why they built the city where they did."

"What's that?"

"Some distance from the astron bed they had discovered a hole in the floor of the ocean."

"What's so odd about that?"

Elanna hesitated and leaned close to Billy. "It was bottomless."

"What?"

"It had no bottom. At least they could never find one, no matter how far down they swam. Mind you, there was a limit to how deep they could go."

"Water pressure," ventured Billy excitedly.

"That's right. And that's why they spent all their lives trying to build different machines that could be lowered into the pool."

"Did they ever get to the bottom?"

"They never did. But they wanted to very badly. They believed that if they went deep enough they would come out on the other side of our planet and maybe find the fuel they could never find up here and—"

"And get back home again!" Billy added.

Elanna nodded and folded her arms like Billy.

"Boy, what a story," he sighed. "What happened to them?"

"The Mad Queen had them all killed."

"Oh, no!"

"When Father banished her and all her people she fled by ski-car to the one place she felt she would be absolutely safe—the city of Mordra. She tricked the fish people into thinking she had come to help them, had them all killed and then pumped the water out of the city and opened up the mines for her astron bricks."

"Wow!" exclaimed Billy. "How could someone who is mad do all that?"

"Well, she wasn't quite as mad then as she is now and she had thousands of followers. Mother used to say she was the most brilliant person she had ever known. I guess hating father the way she did—always plotting against him and living in that terrible place—made her go completely mad. They say she has to be carried around in a cage and that she's sometimes calm but never for long. She screams and yells all the time. It must be awful to see her like that."

Billy trembled visibly. "Whew!" he breathed. "What a spooky story. I'm glad we're here and not with Yan."

Elanna thought for a moment, trying to decide whether or not to continue. Finally she said, "That's not quite the whole story. There's something more."

Billy glanced up sharply. "Oh?"

"What I said wasn't quite true."

"What do you mean?"

"I mean about the queen killing all the fish people."

Billy's eyes narrowed. "You mean she didn't kill *all* of them?"

"Well, almost all, but not quite."

Billy shook his head in puzzlement. "I don't follow you, Elanna."

The Princess looked away. "I shouldn't tell you this because—well, because it's not very nice to hear. Besides, I can't be absolutely certain it's true."

"What is?"

"The story about the Mad Queen's keeping one fish man a prisoner. I've heard that she has him in the bottomless pool and that he's kept pretty hungry and angry. He's not allowed any astron, but he is fed—something else. You can guess what that is."

Billy's face went white. "Oh, no!"

"I saw a picture of a fish man once in a special room in our Museum of History. I never want to see it again. That's why I didn't take you there. It had the most horrible head and body I have ever seen in my life. It gave me nightmares." She paused and studied her friend's face carefully. "I'm sorry, Billy. I didn't want to tell you. I shouldn't have. Not here! Anyway, it's probably only a story."

Billy and Elanna had been so engrossed in the weird tale of the fish man that they had not noticed that the green glow in the crystal had gone out. Now suddenly they became aware of the darkness in the ski-car. They sat gazing numbly at the crystal's dead face. What they had not allowed themselves to believe could happen had happened! Yan and his fifteen commandos had been captured by the Mad Queen. There was no other explanation.

They had their orders from Yan. As junior soldiers they knew exactly what they had to do: fly straight home to King Farron so that a rescue mission could be sent to Mordra.

But they did not move. They stared at the dull crystal. "Are you thinking what—what I'm thinking?" whispered Billy to Elanna after a long silence.

She did not reply right away. "Yes, Billy," she said finally, "but—"

"But what?"

"We promised."

Billy shifted uneasily and frowned. He began to drum his fingers on the arm of the seat. "I know we did—but we didn't know we'd—we'd feel like this if it ever happened."

The Princess nodded slowly.

"We just can't *leave* them," he said, trembling.

The Princess smiled as bravely as she could. "I know we can't."

"If—if we go all the way back to your dad it—it might be too late."

They fell silent and Elanna knew that Billy's mind was dwelling on the vast black city with its evil green windows and the bottomless pool with the monster fish man. She cupped her hand over his and leaned close. There were tears in her eyes but she mustered a smile as she spoke. "Anyway—we don't have anything to worry about. We're only children. The Mad Queen will have too much on her mind even to bother noticing a—a—"

"A couple of kids."

Then Billy did something he had never done before in his whole life. He leaned forward in the semi-darkness and kissed Princess Elanna on the cheek. He fancied he blushed as he did so, but he never knew for sure. Neither did the Princess. It was too dark to tell.

Then they both moved like lightning.

13
The City Beneath the Sea

Spires and towers, black walls and eerie lights loomed ever closer as Billy and Elanna followed the curving roadbed toward Mordra. Straight ahead they could just make out the main gate, which was not unlike the entrance to the quarry.

They were nervous, but confident that once they gained admittance to the underwater city they would be able to move about relatively unnoticed. Dressed in old green coveralls and mining helmets which they had found in a closet at the rear of their ski-car, they felt they had a fairly good disguise. The helmets wobbled a bit on their heads when they turned too quickly and the sleeves and pant legs had to be rolled up, but there was nothing they could do about it except hope that no one would notice.

"This one had better be automatic too," said Elanna, studying the approaching gate.

"Right!" Billy agreed.

It was. Soon they were in a water chamber like the one at the mine. After it emptied, another door slid back, allowing their ski-car to glide into a bright rotunda which led to a long, gloomy central tunnel.

There was no one in sight, so they proceeded along, passing a number of side tunnels whose entrances made them look even gloomier than the one they were in. Neither spoke until they came to a junction where three tunnels forked off in different directions. Billy lifted his foot from the pedal and the car came to a stop.

"Where to now?" he asked half aloud, looking around and wiping perspiration from his brow.

"I guess we'll have to try each in turn and see what we find," Elanna replied, looking anxiously ahead. "Have you noticed how quiet everything is? And we haven't seen any other ski-cars."

"It is strange," Billy agreed. "And this is supposed to be a city."

Selecting the tunnel directly to their right, they glided along it for some distance, finding it no different from the one they had left behind.

Suddenly Elanna exclaimed, "What was that, Billy?"

Billy pulled to a quick stop. "What was what?"

"That light! Didn't you see it?"

"No," he said, and then, "What kind of light?"

"A green one. It flashed and then went away."

Billy looked up and down the empty tunnel. Only the dull glow of crystals in the ceiling greeted him.

"Where did it come from?"

"I don't know," she whispered, "but I know I saw it."

They drove on a short distance and came to another circular area with five tunnels branching off in all directions. It was here, for the first time, that a dreadful thought occurred to them.

"Are you thinking the same thing I am?" whispered Elanna.

Billy nodded his helmeted head several times very slowly. In their eagerness to enter the underwater city and rescue Yan and the others they had not for a second considered the possibility of getting lost.

"It's like a—like a maze," he said finally.

They sat in silence, each mindful of the situation they could find themselves in if they weren't careful, and desperately trying not to panic. For Princess Elanna it was the first time she had ever experienced this kind of fear. For Billy it was the second. Once, when very young, he had strayed into the woods beyond Oak Street and lost his way. His father had had to come and find him. But this time there was no help on the way. The thought of the importance of their mission and the responsibility resting on their shoulders was the only thing that kept them from losing control.

At last, without a word, Billy again selected the tunnel on their right and entered it. They soon came to yet another circular area, but one with only two tunnels leading from it, and for the third time Billy picked the tunnel to the right. At the very least he could be sure of finding his way back to the entrance if they didn't locate Yan.

They had not travelled very far down this tunnel when Elanna again exclaimed that she had seen a flash of green light. This time Billy saw it too. It came from the shelf where he had placed Yan's mysterious crystal.

Elanna picked up the crystal, but there was not the slightest glow. She handed it to Billy.

"I'm sure it was the crystal," he said excitedly.

"Me too, Billy. Do you think it was a signal?"

"Let's keep going and see what happens."

"Remember what Yan told us. He said Father would know what to do with it."

Not long afterward the crystal flashed again and very soon it began to glow with increasing regularity —on, off, on, off—until, to the delight of both children, it burned a steady green.

"Stop the ski-car, Billy!" exclaimed the Princess.

Billy slipped the car into a small side passage where it wouldn't be noticed and the pair stepped out. There was still nothing in sight up or down the tunnel, nor were there any sounds. The heat was intense.

"Come over here," called Elanna from the far side of the tunnel.

Billy joined her and saw that she had discovered a narrow passageway leading off the main corridor. The crystal in his hand began to glow an even brighter green.

"This has to be where Yan is!" whispered Elanna excitedly.

"Shhh!" said Billy, looking up the dark passageway and back over his shoulder. "Yan may be a prisoner and there might be someone watching."

But carefully as they looked they could see no one. Feeling more confident they clasped hands and moved cautiously down the narrow corridor. With every step the crystal grew brighter until at last they reached a stone doorway.

Elanna and Billy looked at each other in the weird glow. Too excited to speak, they touched the smooth stone surface and pressed. Easily, without a sound, the door slid open to reveal a pitch-black chamber. Again the pair looked nervously at each other before advancing. They both wanted to rush back to the security of their ski-car, but they knew that no matter how frightened they were they had to go on. They were too close to finding Yan to turn back now. Biting their lips they stepped inside.

How large the chamber was they couldn't tell because the green crystal did not permit them to see very far. Cautiously they began to follow one of the walls away from the doorway, moving slowly and keeping their hands outstretched so that they would not bump into anything.

Abruptly Billy stopped and gripped Elanna's arm.

"What is it?" she whispered nervously.

"I've—I've touched something."

Trembling with fright he stretched the green crystal as far ahead as he could. In the darkness they could see the figure of a man standing before them. Billy lifted the crystal up toward the face.

"Yan!" they both yelled in delight.

And indeed it was.

Glad beyond words to be with their friend once more, they rushed forward. But Yan did not speak. He remained standing there, absolutely still.

"Yan!" repeated Elanna. "It's us!"

Billy held the glowing crystal very close to their friend's face and touched his cheek. But it was as cold and hard as marble. "He's—he's been frozen with an ice-gun," he stammered, stepping back and putting his arm around Elanna.

The Princess shuddered. "Billy—let's get back to the ski-car as fast as we can!"

They turned and ran straight into a second figure

in the dark chamber. This figure was not frozen. It was, in fact, very much alive.

"We meet again," a familiar voice said as a hand reached out and grasped Billy's arm. There in the green glow of the crystal were the cruel features of the man with the narrow face.

A sharp command rang out and crystals began to glow in clusters from the ceiling. Elanna took a quick, nervous look at the man before them and then at Billy.

"Is this the—the—" she asked.

"Yes," he answered. "The man who—who kidnapped Prince Ladrion."

"Oh," she said, hardly breathing.

"Don't be alarmed," the man said with a thin smile. "No harm has come to your brother."

"Where is he?" demanded Elanna.

"He's quite safe. You'll see him shortly."

A dozen soldiers moved out from the walls of the chamber and stood waiting for the next command. Billy watched them nervously, then looked at Yan. He was so still and looked so strange. Behind him stood the other commandos, lined up like statues. The expedition to rescue Prince Ladrion had been a total disaster. All had been captured.

"Don't be so downcast, young fellow," the tall man said, smiling. Billy noticed he was wearing a pair of Azidor's special earrings, no doubt taken from one of the King's soldiers. "You ought to be quite pleased, really. You arrived just in time to join in the Queen's Games. By the way, I'm Colonel Zor. And you?"

"Billy Brown," whispered Billy, his voice going strangely hoarse.

"I was right the first time we met, wasn't I? You do come from another world, somewhere far beyond Zomar?"

"Yes," said Billy, not knowing what else to say.

The Colonel smiled and rubbed his hands together. "How very interesting. We must have a long chat later. Both the Queen and I will have many questions to ask you. We are particularly interested in that flying globe you used when you escaped from me in the forest—the device you no doubt used to get to Zomar in the first place."

"F-f-flying globe?" stammered Billy.

"Yes, young man, flying globe—bubbleship—whatever you call it. Don't tell me you have forgotten so soon? You used it to get through the ocean to Mordra, didn't you? All of you." He laughed. "On your *surprise* attack." He laughed again. "Never mind. We'll get the secret out of you later. One of you will talk. All in due time. Such devices will be very useful to the Queen." He clapped his gloved hands and strode toward the door. "Now take off those ridiculous coveralls and helmets and come along. The Queen mustn't be kept waiting."

While the children changed, Colonel Zor barked instructions to his soldiers. "The Games will be starting very shortly." His arm darted toward Yan and the others. "You know where to take them and what to do with them. Move!"

The Colonel walked so swiftly down the passageway to the main tunnel that Billy and Elanna had to run to keep up with him. Without noticing the ski-car hidden in its dark tunnel he walked directly to the far wall and pressed a tiny button. Two panels slid open revealing an elevator platform. Zor motioned impatiently for the children to step in with him and then the panels closed. Billy could detect no motion whatever, but a few moments later the panels opened again and they found themselves in a hall of glistening black marble where windows looked out into the dim green depths of the ocean.

"By the way," asked the Colonel, glancing down at Billy, "do you play chess?"

Billy nodded, wondering why he would ask such a question.

"Excellent!" cried the Colonel as he ushered his captives through a pair of silver-coloured doors at the end of the hall.

The chamber was deep with a long set of steps leading down to a large table at the bottom. All around, running in giant circles, were narrow aisles with seats and desks. It looked like a lecture room.

"This way," commanded the Colonel, striding down the steps. At the bottom he moved through an exit. "In here."

The room in which they were now standing was pure white and contained something that made Princess Elanna's eyes sparkle.

"Ladrion!" she shouted, rushing forward to embrace a boy with tousled red hair who lay upon a table apparently asleep. She cradled his head in her arms and pressed her cheek to his, crying and laughing at the same time.

"He's resting," a voice said from one side of the room, "and cannot be awakened just yet."

Billy turned and gazed, mesmerized, at a woman sitting on a golden throne. With her long black hair and her lovely face set off by a flaming red gown, she was the most beautiful woman he had ever seen. She beckoned to him with slender fingers adorned with golden rings.

"Come closer and let me look at you," she said. Her voice was soft and gentle.

Who could this be? wondered Billy. Elanna and Yan had never told him about this woman. She was most certainly not the Mad Queen.

But as he approached the throne he noticed handles protruding from its arms, and behind it, not visible until now because it stood in an alcove, he saw something that made his heart sink. It was a cage of gold with four uniformed women guarding it.

14
The Mad Queen

"Do you know who I am?" asked the beautiful woman on the throne.

Billy nodded slowly. Impossible though it seemed, he knew he was face to face with the Mad Queen.

"I'll pardon you for not kneeling," she smiled. "But just this once. Everything must be very strange for you. Colonel Zor tells me you come from another world. How fascinating! He also tells me you travel in a most interesting way. Well, you will have much to tell us during your long stay here in Mordra."

Billy's ears tingled at the word *long,* and yet the eyes he looked into were so soft and blue that he could not for a moment imagine them capable of the wickedness he had been told about. They were more like pools, deep and peaceful, and he felt himself drawn into them. But the trance was momentary. The eyes narrowed, seemed to change to a greenish colour, then glanced away from Billy to the Princess.

"You may approach me, Elanna," the Mad Queen said.

The Princess knelt before the Queen, then rose. Her cheeks were still stained with tears.

"My, my!" said the Queen, reaching forward and dabbing Elanna's face with a handkerchief. "You are so pretty. So very much like your mother. But you mustn't cry. No harm has come to Prince Ladrion and no harm will come to you. He has been put to sleep for a little while. He will awaken soon." She sat back in her chair, looking happy and radiant.

Billy was now quite certain that all would be well. The Mad Queen, whatever had been the cause of her madness, was obviously cured. But from the expression on Princess Elanna's face he could see she wasn't as easily convinced as he was.

The Princess bit her lip, took a deep breath and said in a voice that was scarcely above a whisper, "What are you going to do to Ladrion?"

The Queen rose, crossed the floor to the table where the Prince lay, and gazed down at him thoughtfully. "I had him brought here to give him a gift," she replied, "a gift no one would ever know he possessed."

Billy was now no longer certain the Queen was cured of her madness. She seemed to be speaking in riddles.

She clapped her hands twice and a woman dressed in white entered carrying a small metal box which she placed on the table beside Ladrion. Motioning to Elanna and Billy to look, the Queen opened the lid. They could see nothing but a tiny crystal lying on a green cloth.

"They look puzzled, Your Majesty," chuckled Colonel Zor.

The Queen snapped her fingers and was handed a pair of tweezers by the woman in white. She picked up the crystal and held it up to the light. It glistened and twinkled like a star far off in space.

"What is that for?" asked Billy nervously.

"It is the gift I am going to give Prince Ladrion. Don't you like it?"

"What—what is it?"

The Queen smiled benignly. "Something that your wise Azidor would never even dream of inventing. Something miraculous. Something that could only have come from my scientists here in Mordra."

She placed the tiny crystal on Prince Ladrion's forehead. "Right after the Games we will come back here for the operation. My surgeon will place this crystal inside the Prince's forehead. It will be painless. He will never know he has it. Then the Colonel will take him home to Vensor where you, Billy, and Princess Elanna had so much fun tobogganing. You didn't know I knew that, did you?"

The two children looked at each other in astonishment. So the Queen's eyes were everywhere!

"When Prince Ladrion regains consciousness he will remember nothing, neither the Colonel nor me, nor the fact that you and Yan are my guests here in Mordra. He will tell your father what we want him to tell him."

"Father won't believe him," burst in Elanna. "He'll know we're prisoners and he'll send his army to rescue us!"

"Of course he will want to do that—eventually. But before he does, Ladrion will ask your father the questions that we want him to ask. And all the answers will come back to us here." She tapped the Prince's forehead with the tweezers. "From this tiny crystal."

"What questions? What answers?" asked Elanna in alarm.

"Oh," said the Mad Queen, returning to her throne, "where your father's outposts are—and how many soldiers are in each. What parts of the coast are unprotected. Where the new ice-gun factories are located. Things like that. Everything that Prince Ladrion sees and hears will be fed back to our laboratory."

It did not take a military expert to know the reason for wanting this kind of information and Billy blurted it out without even thinking.

"You're going to try to capture Zomara!"

"Excellent!" exclaimed the Colonel, rubbing his hands together with delight. "Excellent! But we are going to do better than try!"

"And of course we will learn all about your father's plans to rescue you before his mission even gets started," chuckled the Queen. "That's why the Colonel and I felt there would be no harm in revealing our little secrets to you. We'll soon have a fine collection of your soldiers captured right here in Mordra." She chuckled again, sighed and began pacing the room. "Later, when I have returned to Zomara and have overthrown your father, you can come home, Elanna. You and Ladrion will be together again and can play as long and happily as you want. You have my word."

"But we'll still be your prisoners!" exclaimed the Princess, horrified. "And what will happen to Father and—and to Billy?"

"Nothing, my child, nothing. I am merciful. You'll be able to visit your father here once in a while."

"Here?" repeated Elanna.

"Yes, here. A charming place, quite suited to a

royal mind. As well as a place where we can keep an eye on him. No one has ever escaped from Mordra, my dear, and," she laughed, "no one ever will."

"And Billy?"

"Ah yes, Billy." She studied the boy, a puzzled look in her green eyes, then reached over and drew him to her. "I have so many questions to ask our visitor, so much to learn. I think I shall keep Billy very, very close to me." She patted his head gently and smiled tenderly. The colour of her eyes changed to an infinite blue.

Then she turned to the woman in white and with one wave of her hand abruptly changed the mood of the room. "Have everything ready for the operation following the Games. I don't want to waste a moment." The woman bowed and turned to attend to Prince Ladrion. "And," continued the Queen, looking sharply at the Colonel, "you will be prepared to depart with the Prince immediately afterward."

The Colonel smiled. "I am ready, Your Majesty."

"Good! Now you can escort the children to the arena. Oh, by the way, do you play chess where you come from, Billy?"

"I've already inquired," put in Colonel Zor, grinning, "and he does."

"Splendid! Splendid!" said the Queen. "The children couldn't have timed their arrival better. We'll all have such fun!" With that she swept off through an exit, waving her attendants to follow.

* * *

The balcony in which Billy and Elanna now found themselves was located above an arena containing a gigantic board of black and white squares. Tiers of seats rose up around the board and these were filled with people wearing colourful tunics and hats. From the din of the crowd the children knew that, whatever the Queen's Games were, the citizens of Mordra were looking forward to them with considerable excitement.

High above their heads, set in the curved ceiling directly over the board, was a stack of large metal plates with long ropes running up to them from each balcony. Billy wondered what they were for and Elanna explained that they were probably astron-vents. By pulling or slackening the ropes the Queen's servants could control the air in the arena.

This satisfied Billy's curiosity only momentarily, for next he was pointing to a strange device on the balcony immediately opposite.

"That's an ice-gun, Billy," whispered the Princess.

Billy whistled through his teeth. "Boy, it's big! And it's aimed down at the board. I wonder why?"

"I don't know."

"I wish I knew what kind of games are going to be played."

"Still plotting?" sneered Colonel Zor. "It won't do you any good, you know. You got away from me once, but not a second time. There's no place you can hide in Mordra. The Queen sees everything in the city."

Billy hardly heard what Zor was saying, so intent was he on trying to imagine what kind of game would be played on such a large board. Finally he remembered the question both the Colonel and the Queen had asked him earlier and the obvious struck him.

"Do you play chess, Elanna?"

"Father and Ladrion used to," she answered.

Billy nodded. So does the Mad Queen, he thought. But here? The pieces would have to be enormous.

They were. In the next few minutes a long file of attendants entered the arena carrying huge chess pieces. The pieces were as large as human beings and were so lifelike that—

Billy's mind stopped in mid-thought and his throat tightened. He nudged Elanna and motioned with his head toward the far side of the board.

"Oh, no!" gasped the Princess.

One by one Yan and his fifteen commandos— wearing crowns and spears and appropriate white costumes—were being placed on the board in chess formation.

Colonel Zor seemed to be enjoying the activity immensely. He leaned over to the children. "They make admirable chess pieces, don't you think?" he chuckled. Billy and Elanna were too appalled by the strangeness of what was happening to respond. The Colonel studied their faces for a moment and added, "You still don't understand what's going on, do you?"

"They will very shortly," exclaimed a voice from the doorway behind. It was the Mad Queen. She was seated in her golden cage which was being carried onto the balcony by attendants. When the litter was lowered and the door opened she stepped out and joined Colonel Zor and the children by the railing. Immediately hysterical cheers broke from the crowds below and a band struck up the Mordrian national anthem, which brought everyone to their feet.

When the anthem finished, the Queen signalled the crowd to be seated, then motioned for her chess team to enter. Sixteen men and women, clad in black and appropriately costumed, entered the arena and took their positions on the board. This ritual was accompanied by loud cheering from the crowds and blaring music from the band.

The Queen leaned over to Billy with a friendly

smile. There was no trace whatever of the hysterical, screaming creature he had been led to expect. "We will start our first game in a moment, but first I want to show you both something interesting." She motioned with her hand. "Look over the railing, children, straight down. I think you'll be amused by what you see."

Billy and Elanna did as they were told and found they were looking down on a circular pool of dark green water extending from the near side of the great chessboard. The pool was absolutely calm, but something—and this made Billy and Elanna gasp—something was gliding in circles beneath its surface. It was long and green and scaly, and its head... The children quickly averted their eyes and looked aghast at the Queen.

"That's where the white pieces go as they are captured during the game." The Queen smiled. "Are you sure you don't want to see more?"

They shook their heads.

"What a pity." Her face darkened and her eyes flared green. "We find it quite entertaining." Next she pointed toward another part of the arena and her face brightened. "Do you see where those tables and chairs are? That's where the black pieces go if they are captured."

The children could not quite grasp what she was saying.

"They have tea and cakes there while they wait for the game to end. Not quite—shall we say—as exciting as being dropped into the pool, is it? And not very fair? No, I grant you that." Her voice was merry. "But then, I've never claimed my chess games were fair, have I, Colonel Zor?"

The Colonel smiled.

"Any more than life is fair," she continued, laughing in a strangely silent way. Then she stood erect and clapped her hands together.

"Let the first game begin!"

15

The Chess Game

When the band finished playing a lively fanfare a table and two chairs were brought forward and placed between the Queen and Billy. Billy looked puzzled and Elanna's brow furrowed, but the Queen was positively radiant. The table appeared quite normal except for the fact that the tips of its legs were made of crystal and fitted into four slots in the balcony floor. The attendants tested the table to make sure it was snug and steady.

By now Billy was thoroughly alarmed.

A crystal chess board complete with carved, crystal figures was placed on the table. Small metal shafts extended from the bottom of the board and these fitted into sockets in the table top.

"Now, Master Billy," smiled the Queen, "we will play chess! Yes—you and I!"

Billy gasped.

"Don't look so startled. You are a visitor from

space. You are therefore a most celebrated guest in my city. I hope you appreciate the honour I am bestowing upon you by inviting you to play with me. Normally Colonel Zor plays the opening game, using prisoners from our dungeons."

The Colonel bowed and shrugged generously.

While two attendants arranged the Queen's dress so that it would not crease when she sat down, another pair motioned Billy to his chair. He was too horrified to resist. He tried to speak, but words would not come. The situation was unbelievable. He was going to have to play chess for the lives of Yan and his commandos! If he made a wrong move . . . if he lost . . .

A loud cheering broke from the crowd in the arena.

"You may make the first move," said the Queen with a cruel smile.

Billy looked pleadingly toward Elanna, but there was nothing she could do. She stared dumbly at her friend.

"Come, come!" urged the Queen. "Your move!"

Billy clenched his teeth, and his hand, like that of a robot, reached out and moved his king's pawn two squares forward.

Immediately, as if by magic, one of Yan's soldiers on the giant board below glided forward two squares.

The game had begun and the crowd roared its approval.

Now it was the Queen's turn. She also moved her king's pawn forward two spaces and one of her soldiers glided into the designated square. Another roar from the crowd, this time followed by applause.

"I'll wager you don't have chessboards like this back home, Billy," the Queen said. "Or you, Elanna."

The children shook their heads grimly.

"I thought as much. The pieces down there have to move the way we move the pieces up here. They have no power." She chuckled. "We have all the power." Her fingers then caressed a circular hole in the chess table through which Billy could see a net or pocket. "Even when we capture pieces and discard them in here, they have no power."

This made Colonel Zor laugh uproariously. Billy glanced down at the terrible green pool with its hideous occupant swimming endlessly in circles—waiting.

He dared not make his next move too quickly. He tried to remember what his father had taught him about strategy and tactics. But this was no ordinary game. There was so much at stake. Billy looked at Yan and the others and a wave of pity swept through him. He had to be careful; he had to concentrate.

He also had to think beyond the game he was playing and plan some means of escape. Whatever he did, it had to be done here in the arena, at the Queen's Games. There would be no hope afterward.

Billy knew he didn't stand a chance playing chess with the Mad Queen. She was too clever. He would have to come up with some kind of trick, some kind of surprise. But what?

He sighed, put his hands behind his head and let his eyes wander to the long rope that stretched from the balcony railing far up to the astron-vent in the ceiling. From there he let his gaze settle on the large ice-gun in the balcony on the far side. A guard was now in position behind it.

The Queen noticed where Billy's attention was directed. "You are wondering why I keep the ice-gun in here?"

Billy nodded casually, not wanting to appear too interested.

She smiled, clapped her hands and pointed toward the chessboard in the arena. The guard on the far balcony saluted, took aim, then pressed a large red button on the side of the gun. A red ray shot downward and immediately Yan snapped back to life on his chessboard square. He stood dazed, not knowing where he was. Billy and Elanna could have cheered for joy at the sight of their old friend alive once more, but the Queen clapped her hands a second time and the guard pressed a white button. There was a streak of white light and Yan was instantly frozen again—a fragile glass figure that would shatter into a thousand pieces if it ever fell over.

The Queen broke Billy's trance. "Naturally when I capture your chessmen I don't want to send them down *there*"—she pointed toward the pool below— "without their knowing where they are going or what is happening to them." She laughed cruelly. "They would miss all the fun!" Then she laughed again, but more excitedly, and Billy noticed a strange look come into her eyes. In a flash he knew that everything he had heard about the Queen was true.

That gave him an idea.

If he could do something surprising, absurd, outrageous, something that would make the Queen go really mad—madder than she had ever been before— everyone's attention would be on her. That just might give him enough time to ...

Billy cupped his hand to his chin, shook his head slowly and narrowed his eyes to suggest deep, deep thought. Not that he wasn't thinking. He was thinking very hard. But he wanted to make the Queen believe he was concentrating only on the game.

Chuckling at the frown on Billy's forehead the Queen whispered a joking remark to Colonel Zor.

She was thrilled that her first move had produced such an effect on the boy.

Billy shook his head, got up and stood by the railing, stretching his arms as though his muscles were tight. He took several deep breaths. The crowd below sat hushed, waiting for the next move. Huge, ugly fish were staring with saucer eyes into the stadium from the large crystal window at the far end of the arena as though they too were waiting for the move.

The Mad Queen grew impatient. "Come along, Billy," she commanded. "We've only just started to play. It's your move!"

Colonel Zor tapped Billy on the shoulder as a gentle reminder. Princess Elanna bit her lip, desperately wondering what Billy was going to do next. She knew he was up to something—but what?

Billy sighed and sat down once more. Casually, almost as though he were bored, he moved the king's bishop diagonally three squares. And on the large chessboard the frozen figure of one of Yan's soldiers glided into position.

Although no one would have guessed it from the look on his face—least of all the Queen, who had grown impatient over the delay—Billy was attempting a most desperate gamble. It was a tricky little play his father had taught him called a "fool's mate." If she didn't notice in time he could defeat the Queen in the next two moves. Such a shocking and disastrous event for Her Majesty might just provide Billy and his friends with the chance they needed.

"I certainly didn't think you would be such a slow player," the Queen grumbled, barely waiting for him to put his piece into place before moving her queen's knight. "There now, my little friend, let's see what you will do with that." She laughed quite loudly, almost hysterically, and glanced at the admiring Colonel.

Billy caught the queer, unbalanced look on her face and decided it was now or never. Looking worried and more than a little hesitant—an expression that added considerably to the Mad Queen's feeling of superiority—he moved his queen diagonally two squares. Then he muttered something under his breath as though suddenly realizing he had made a bad move.

The Queen laughed to see him under such pressure. Her abundant confidence in her own ability caused her to make her next move very quickly. She moved her bishop three squares diagonally.

This kind of move was precisely what Billy had counted on. With great calmness he moved his queen directly forward four spaces and captured the pawn next to the Mad Queen's king. "Check!" he whispered in a barely audible voice. "And I think..."

But he did not say "mate." He did not have to.

For a split second there was dead silence on the balcony as the Queen tried to comprehend what had just happened. Then, stammering and foaming at the corners of her mouth, she half rose from her chair and pointed a quivering hand at Billy. But words would not come. Even Colonel Zor was speechless.

An angry roar shot up from the arena as the crowd realized that in three simple moves Billy had won.

The Queen leaped up and grasped the railing, her mouth still opening and closing with no sounds coming out. But Billy had one more blow to strike at her pride. Rising to his feet so that everyone could see him clearly he shouted, "Checkmate!" and again, "Checkmate!"

This was the final straw. No one had ever said checkmate to the Queen, under any circumstances! Only the Queen said checkmate! Only the Queen won at chess! No one ever insulted the Queen! No one ever tricked her in front of her people! No one ever . . .

Her mind snapped completely. Body writhing in twisting, wrenching convulsions, she uttered the most horrifying screams. Turning away from the children, she struggled across the balcony, clawing at the archway for support. But the shuddering jerks were too much for her. Slowly she sank to her knees, her fingers tearing at her lovely black hair, her voice shrieking insanely. Up to this point her back had been turned to Elanna and Billy and they could not see her face, but now she turned toward the children and glared at them in full fury. Her face was ghastly, terrifying. Flaming red eyes burned like hot irons above a gnashing, snarling mouth. Her tongue darted out and in like a snake's and the shrieking pitch of her voice rose higher and higher until Elanna thought her eardrums would burst.

Colonel Zor leaped to her aid and tried to bring her under control, but she clawed and banged at him and tried to push him over the railing. Instantly her four attendants were upon her, trying to pull her away from the Colonel and get her into the golden cage. But the Mad Queen was having none of it. In a wild, insane rage she fought back with the strength of a tiger.

Suddenly Elanna felt an arm around her waist and found herself being pulled to the doorway where guards and servants were streaming through in crazy confusion.

"Wait here," Billy whispered. "I'm going to try something."

Elanna grabbed his hand before he could move away. "Do you want me to get Ladrion?" she asked urgently. "I'll bring him here!"

Billy looked into her eyes. "You'd never make it! They'd never let you!"

"I'll try," she said, giving his arm a squeeze.

"But what if you can't get back?"

Elanna thought for a moment. "I know what I'll do. I'll hide in the ski-car. No one would ever think of looking there!" In the next moment she had darted out the door and was gone.

Billy did not try to hold her. Time was too precious. He ran to the far end of the balcony and before the Colonel could collect his wits in the turmoil surrounding the Queen's cage he had undone the end of the long rope and leaped from the railing.

The swing was not unlike that awful flight across the river and its ending was just as sudden. Billy swooped down over the heads of the confused crowd, then up to the balcony on the far side, flying with a thud into the ice-gun operator. The blow knocked the man against the stone wall where he collapsed unconscious.

Colonel Zor had yanked the chess table out of its floor sockets so that the circuit used to control the chess pieces would be broken. "Stop him!" he screamed to the soldiers on the chessboard, his voice rising above the roar of the crowd and the raging shrieks of the Mad Queen who had still not been put into her cage. The Queen's chessmen streamed into a side exit where stairs led to the balcony above. Zor waved his ice-pistol and fired wildly at Billy.

With only seconds to accomplish everything he had planned, Billy jumped behind the ice-gun, punched the red button as he had seen the operator do, and sent a red ray darting across Yan's frozen commandos on the chessboard!

16
The Battle

Instantly Billy's friends were restored to life, amazed to discover where they were but already moving into action. It took Yan only a glance to size up the situation. Yelling a command to his soldiers, he swung a chair over his head and charged directly into the squad of guards pushing through the main entrance.

By the time the guards burst onto the balcony Billy had the ice-gun swung around and trained on the archway. The first were frozen in their tracks in the narrow opening, slowing the progress of the others behind. A few tumbled over and shattered into fragments on the floor.

So far Billy's tactics had been brilliant, but he had forgotten one thing. In turning the giant ice-gun to fire at the archway he had exposed himself to the Colonel, who had been trying unsuccessfully to get a clear shot at him.

Now Zor had his chance and the old villainous smile returned to his thin lips. Leaning far out over the balcony railing to keep his gun arm free of the jostling throng behind him, he carefully took aim at Billy's back. There was nothing between them. "Farewell, my little man," he muttered softly as he pressed the white button on his ice-gun.

But despite the pressure he thought he was applying, his finger never moved. For a split second he wondered why. The Colonel never saw the burst of light from the ice-gun that had stopped him before he could fire. Like a toppled statue his frozen figure lost its balance and fell over the balcony railing, plunging into the depths of the green pool.

On the far side of the chessboard Yan smiled with grim satisfaction at the splash, then trained his ice-gun on a fresh wave of incoming guards.

By now the Mad Queen had been successfully caged by her guards, and even though her shrieking had not ceased, she was able to follow the dark tide of battle raging before her. Seeing that Yan's soldiers and Billy were more than a match for her troops, she pointed hysterically and screamed commands to her guards, along with terrible threats if they failed.

To Billy's horror the battle began to change in the Queen's favour as more and more soldiers poured into the arena. He could think of only one last desperate thing to try. It was a pure gamble.

Swinging his ice-gun around, he aimed at the great ocean window at the end of the arena. Clenching his teeth and bracing his body against the impact, he fired. For all he knew the ice-ray would pass right through the window and fade into the green depths.

It didn't.

A large circle in the window, made suddenly fragile by the ice-ray, gave way to the enormous pressure behind it and a mammoth jet of water spouted into the arena, sweeping everything before it.

Inhaling deeply, Billy dipped his plastic loop into the mouth of his canteen and gave a long, full blow. Immediately a string of bubbles flew down to where Yan and his squad were fighting in a tight circle with the rising water gushing around them.

"The bubbles, Yan! The bubbles!" Billy screamed above the din.

Sirens began to wail throughout the city, warning everyone that a leak had occurred. The soldiers on the staircase, who had been trying to get through the clogged balcony archway to capture Billy, scrambled for the nearest exit. Some made it on foot or were washed through to safety in the corridors beyond, but most were trapped in the swirling deluge inside the arena.

The last to depart was the Mad Queen. She insisted that her attendants leave her on the balcony as long as possible, hopeful that she might be able to wreak some final, dreadful vengeance on Billy. But when the water rose up to the railing and whirled dangerously around her she reluctantly agreed to be carried out. Giving Billy a violent shake of her clenched fist and a vicious glare from her flaming eyes, she left. The door slid shut behind her with a hollow *boom* and her strange, dark, mad, beautiful image was gone.

Swiftly Billy blew one final bubble. As he descended toward Yan and his soldiers a cold chill of horror ran from the tips of his toes to the roots of his hair. Something had swept in front of him, blocking his friends from view—something enormously long and covered all over with green scales. It had the weaving tail and fins of a fish, but the claw-like hands and hooded yellow eyes of a lizard. It was the fish man from the bottomless pool and it was swimming straight for Billy!

For a moment the creature hovered in front of him. Then to his unutterable relief it shot past, almost brushing the bubble with its tail, and streaked toward two of the Queen's chessmen who were trying to swim to the surface.

Billy did not linger to see what the fish man would do to them. He dived on toward Yan whose bubble was hovering near the ocean window which by now had blown out entirely. The figures of the other commandos were dimly visible in the green depths outside.

"Come on!" shouted Yan, his voice sounding faint through the water.

Quickly Billy moved his bubble close to Yan's so that they could talk. "I can't go without Elanna," he said breathlessly. "She went for Ladrion! She was supposed to come back but she hasn't. I've got to get in there, Yan! I've got to get in there somehow and find her!"

"It's too risky," Yan said, "much too risky. I can't let you do it. You'll never make it alone."

"It's the only way, Yan, believe me. I won't be spotted. There's too much going on. Anyway, if anything happens you'll still be able to rescue me because you'll be on the outside. At least we won't both be caught!"

Yan knew from the look in Billy's eyes that any further argument was useless. He also knew there was no time to waste. Turning to his men, whose bubbles now clustered tightly around the open window, he shouted instructions. "I want half of you to remain here in case Billy tries to come out this way. He may need help. The other half can follow me to the ski-car entrance where we came into the city. We'll enter from there if possible. If we don't come out I want those who stayed here to head for Vensor and bring back an army!"

"Don't you think, sir, that some of us should go with Billy?" called one of the soldiers.

"That's what I think, yes, but he has convinced me we'd draw too much attention. Besides, Billy will be able to move faster alone. He knows the way through the tunnels better than we do."

The commandos divided into two groups, one taking up position in the arena, the other waiting for Yan to lead them out along the city wall. Billy scanned the depths for some sign of the fish man, but the creature was nowhere in sight.

"Now let's see if I can get you back into the city," said Yan, the worried look still stamped on his face. The two shot up through the water to one of the sealed balcony doors. But luck was not on their side. Yan had difficulty selecting the right combination of crystals from his pouch and in Billy's nervous state the moments seemed like hours. Was Elanna safe? Had she managed to resuce Prince Ladrion from the operating room and get to the ski-car? Was he making a big mistake going into Mordra alone? Maybe he should have listened to Yan. Billy shivered as he imagined the mischief the Mad Queen might be up to.

"I've almost got it," whispered Yan. He applied a

red and white crystal to the door, rotating it at right angles to the others.

A dull click sounded through the sea water.

"There, that does it. It's ready to open." Yan took out a spare ice-gun and turned to Billy. "I don't want anything to happen to you, so maybe you'd better take this." He pushed the weapon into Billy's bubble. "I've jammed the lock crystals. That'll delay the guards a little, but you won't have much time. You'll have to move fast." He gave Billy one last smile and waved his hand. "Look after yourself. See you at the entrance." With that he dived back toward his men.

Praanngg! The door yielded and Billy burst into the corridor beyond, riding on an enormous torrent of water. Suddenly guards were splashing and scrambling everywhere around him, but they were more concerned with trying to get the door shut than with capturing him.

Billy zoomed toward a stairwell, plunged down it and glided out along a high, broad, black-marble corridor. Water was running in swift streams below him and sirens still echoed throughout the city. People surged through the halls, too frightened to notice the oddity of a boy flying overhead in a shimmering blue bubble.

Another stairwell led to the entrance of the operating theatre. Ice-gun at the ready, Billy opened the door and slipped inside. But the operating room and the small room beyond it were empty. There was no trace of Elanna or Ladrion.

They must have headed for the ski-car, he thought, regaining the corridor—unless the Mad Queen got them first! But he did not want to dwell on that possibility.

At the elevator he had ridden in earlier Billy dismounted and deflated his bubble. Moments later he was on ground level. The long, gloomy tunnel with its overhead clusters of crystal lights curved off in both directions. It was empty.

Apparently none of the guards had discovered the ski-car—it was still parked in the narrow alley where he had hidden it. But of Elanna and Ladrion there was not a sign.

Where could they be?

Billy sank to the tunnel floor, his knees bunched up under his chin, his face a mask of defeat. Suddenly his eye caught sight of something yellow protruding from under the car.

A glove! Prince Ladrion's glove!

Billy was on his feet in a flash. "They were here! They knew I'd follow and left this as a sign. They've probably gone to the entrance." Billy climbed into the ski-car and sped off to the first intersection where tunnels converged.

"I hope I remember the way," he repeated silently

at each turning. But his memory had not slipped. He took the first tunnel to the left at each circle, and in much less time than it had taken on the first trip he found himself rounding the last curve. From the bright glow of crystal lights shining ahead he knew that the giant doors leading to the water chamber were close at hand.

"Please let them be here!" he breathed, crossing his fingers.

They were!

Billy's eyes swam with tears of joy. Elanna and Ladrion were standing together in a pool of crystal light!

But they were not alone. A white ski-car, long and low, with the Royal Crest on its doors, hovered nearby. And someone was stepping out—the Mad Queen.

Almost at once other ski-cars appeared and converged around Billy. Sadly he opened his panel door and stepped down into the circle of light. Grimly he faced the Mad Queen and her guards.

"My turn to checkmate you, Billy Brown!" said the Mad Queen with a terrible laugh.

"Oh, Billy, I'm sorry," called Elanna. "I'm so sorry."

Billy rushed forward and took her hands in his. He tried to smile but couldn't. "We'll be all right, don't worry," he said bravely. Briefly he clasped

Prince Ladrion's shoulder.

"Of course they'll be all right," asserted the Queen. "I never harm children. Not too much. But as for you"—she shot a glance at Billy—"I think an exception is in order. The Colonel was an important man in Mordra. You must pay for what you did, Billy. Pay dearly!"

She waved her men into action. "For now—ice him." She smiled. "Then take him to the dungeons! But be careful how you carry him. I don't want anything missing!" She spun on her heels and stepped toward her ski-car. "Come, children. It's time for tea."

The guards moved slowly into a circle around Billy, their ice-guns drawn. He was powerless. Even speech failed him. Elanna put her hand to her mouth and Ladrion shuddered.

But the Queen's guards did not fire immediately. They were enjoying their moment of triumph too much—like cats surrounding a mouse, knowing they need not hurry because there was no hope for the mouse. Nothing could save Billy now.

A booming *praanngg!* roared through the rotunda as giant metal doors ground open. And there, sweeping in from the water chamber, green seawater flying from their bubbles, came Yan and eight commandos.

The Queen saw them first, but her cry came

too late. Ice-guns spurted from all directions like searchlights gone crazy. Yan and his commandos leapt from their bubbles and flung themselves at the Queen's guards.

"Oh, no!" moaned the Queen, making for the door of her ski-car. As a last desperate measure she tried to carry off Elanna and Ladrion, but they were too much for her. Biting and kicking and pulling her long black hair, they forced the Queen to jump through the panel door alone, leaving her guards lying frozen and shattered like a pile of broken china dolls on the tunnel floor.

In a rush of wind the white ski-car glided away. The last thing anyone heard was a piercing "We'll meet again, Billy Brown! We'll meet again!" echoing down the long, dark tunnel.

Then Billy and Elanna and Ladrion were swept up in Yan's strong arms as a great cheer rose from the bubble commandos.

17
The Return to Nightcross

The parade through the streets of Vensor in honour of the rescue of Prince Ladrion was the most magnificent spectacle Billy had ever seen. But to be part of it—that was almost too much for him. Waving, cheering crowds lined the streets all the way from the blue crystal castle to the old part of the city. They overflowed the stone pavements and jostled wildly to get a better view of the heroes as they passed. From packed balconies overhead came a constant shower of red, white and blue crystal petals, dazzling in the bright sunlight.

At the head of the procession came the King's band playing the national anthem of Zomara—a haunting victory march that made everyone's heart beat faster. Directly behind them in the leading open-air ski-car sat Azidor, smiling and bobbing his ancient head to the crowds with all the delight of a child at a birthday party. He was having a marvellous time turning handfuls of petals into snow and producing birds out of thin air simply by clapping his hands together. The children adored him.

Next came four cars carrying the men and women of Yan's squad—all in dazzling white parade dress and all smiling and waving through the shower of petals.

Following the commandos, sitting by themselves in a splendid car, came King Farron and Prince Ladrion, the father beaming at his son and waving almost absentmindedly at the passing sea of faces.

Finally came the epic touch. It had been designed by Azidor and the sight drove the spectators to a frenzy of emotion. Here at last were Yan, Elanna and Billy — each floating in a shimmering blue bubble hovering before a huge tableau of the terrible underwater city of Mordra. The three smiled and waved at the ecstatic crowd while the Princess's marching band played a rousing fanfare.

"How could you possibly leave us now, Billy?" Yan asked out of the corner of his mouth, moving close to make himself heard over the clamour. "You're a national hero. Every home in the kingdom has your picture. Parents are naming their children after you ..."

"I'd sure like to stay — at least a little while longer," answered Billy, fingering the blue medal of honour that King Farron had hung around his neck in an earlier ceremony in the castle square.

"You know Father and Ladrion don't want you to go, Billy," said Elanna, "and—and—"

Billy diverted his eyes briefly from the crowds. "I know. It won't be easy to say goodbye, not after all we've been through together."

"Then why not stay with us a little longer?"

"I have to go sometime and I've been thinking about Mom and Dad a lot lately, and Steve and Nancy too. I guess I've been getting homesick ever since we got back from Mordra. Funny it didn't happen earlier."

Yan laughed. "You were too busy to think about anything except what was happening here. You're still not worrying about how you're going to get home, are you, Billy?"

"Azidor says he has it all worked out. He knows where the black hole is—at least he's pretty sure he can find the mists over the ocean now that he has a bubble to fly in—and he is certain I can go back home the same way I came."

The other two fell silent, their smiles and waves to the crowd becoming mechanical. They were trying to remain cheerful, but the thought of Billy's departure, which they knew had to come sometime, had begun to dampen their spirits. It was particularly hard on Elanna who had grown to—

The Princess's eyes suddenly went as round as buttons!

"Billy! Wait! What's happening?"

Billy's balloon was beginning to jiggle and jerk as though it were moored to the ground by wires and a big wind was trying to pull it free.

The parade had come to a brief halt and the roar of the crowd was deafening. At first Billy wasn't even aware of what was happening. He was hypnotized by the sight of a mother and father at the edge of the crowd. They were about the age of his own parents and were holding a little boy and girl who must have been as old as Steve and Nancy. The family were all smiling and waving at Billy and presented such a picture of love and tenderness that Billy felt tears welling into his eyes. At that very moment, more than anything in the world, he wished he were home with his mother and father again.

The balloon reacted violently!

Billy still didn't know what was happening when the bubble started to soar up through the canyon of crystal buildings and spires, slowly at first, swooping once or twice, then gaining momentum. All he remembered was being hurled head over heels in crazy somersaults and the sound of Elanna's frantic voice calling his name over and over. Tumbling around

160

him were fleeting images of the city of Vensor, followed by glimpses of the kingdom of Zomara disappearing below him.

By the time Billy had regained an upright position in the bubble and could take stock of what was happening to him he was already enveloped by a swirling white fog and was being whirled around in a great circle by the gravitational force whose grip he remembered only too well. Ahead, through a ragged hole in the mists, he saw what he expected, a whirlpool of absolute darkness rotating in empty space.

The sound of Elanna's voice calling his name was still echoing in his mind as he lost consciousness.

* * *

When Billy saw the first faint lights of Nightcross he whooped for joy—and when he spotted his own house he did a little dance in his spongy bubble. He had been away so long he expected to see snow on the ground. But as he swept lower he was startled to discover he was coming home on a night very much like the crisp, late-fall evening on which he had departed.

Could I have been away an entire year? he wondered as his bubble floated through the moonlight and came to rest on the roof just outside his bedroom window. It seemed almost impossible, but . . .

Billy shivered, wondering what his mom and dad were going to say when he marched in on them alive and well after they had no doubt given up hope of ever seeing him again.

He slipped through his window and stood in his old familiar bedroom once more. It was great to be back! He walked to his bed and ran his hands over the cover. He was suddenly very tired as he realized that in the entire time he had spent in the land of Zomara he had never slept so much as a wink.

"Wait!" he said, half aloud. "What's this?"

The covers were thrown back and his pillow had a large dent in it. Someone had been sleeping in his bed! Who could it be? His parents had never let anyone sleep in his bed before. Not even little Steve or Nancy.

How long had he been away?

Maybe someone new was living in his house!

He waited not another second. "Mom! Dad!" he yelled, running out into the hall and down the stairs. "I'm back! I'm back!"

But all he found in the living room was the family babysitter, Marianne, who had leaped up from her homework at the noise. "What's the matter? You'll wake the children. You're supposed to be in bed, Billy!"

He was thunderstruck. He opened his mouth, but nothing came out.

"And you're all dressed!" continued Marianne, obviously irritated. "You should be in your pyjamas." She took him by the elbow and started to lead him back upstairs to his bedroom.

"Where—where are Mom and Dad?" Billy managed to get out finally. "Aren't they in?"

Marianne stopped on the landing and stared at Billy. She placed her hand on his forehead. "Are you feeling all right?"

He nodded.

"Are you sure there's nothing wrong with you?"

"No. Why?"

"Because you saw your mother not more than twenty minutes ago."

Billy's eyes became moons. "Twenty—twenty minutes ago?"

"When she tucked you in before she went with your father to the Cross Country Skiing meeting."

Billy's head swam. He went back to his bedroom, sat down on his bed and stared at his clock. 9:43. He looked at his watch. It was going again! And it said 9:43!

He flopped back on his pillow.

"You must have had a bad dream," said Marianne, a little more sympathetically. I'll get you a glass of milk and—"

But she didn't finish. She didn't have to. Billy Brown was fast asleep.

"I guess it won't hurt if you sleep in your clothes for once," she said softly.

As Marianne tucked the covers around him she noticed the brightly coloured medal on a ribbon around his neck and wondered what it was for. But by the time she had curled up again with her magazine in front of the applewood fire she had already forgotten all about it.

Elwy Yost

Elwy Yost is probably best known as the enthusiastic host of television's *Saturday Night at the Movies, Magic Shadows* and *Talking Film,* three shows which feature motion pictures within a learning context—indeed, this year he was a finalist in the Best Host category of the Actra Awards. He is also executive producer of all three shows and of *Rough Cuts,* a fourth program dealing with films.

Closely connected with his fascination for motion pictures is his interest in writing. Elwy's first writing experience was in fact a short feature film, *In Between,* which won honourable mention in the 1949 Canadian Film Awards, and his first book, *Magic Moments from the Movies,* a collection of film memories. His first book for children, *Secret of the Lost Empire,* was published in 1980.